SAND IN THE SNOW

SAND
IN THE SNOW

NORBERT DAVIS

ILLUSTRATIONS BY
SAMUEL CAHAN

COVER BY
V.E. PYLES

POPULAR PUBLICATIONS · 2023

TABLE OF CONTENTS

SAND IN THE SNOW

California has snow-capped peaks and burning sandy wastes—and Jim Daniels, following the threads of the strangest case he ever undertook, found that sudden and violent death was apt to occur in both climates. In fact, peril seemed to travel in the wake of the Young Millionaire with the Scarred Face, ready to pounce at any moment. An exciting novel of a brilliant young attorney's midwinter vacation from safety.

1

THE LADY TAKES A GUN

IT WAS HIS wife's mink coat that started the whole thing. Jim Daniels had no reason to get mad about it. Ordinarily he wouldn't have. It just came at the wrong time. He admitted all that later, but by then it was too late. The ball was already rolling down its swift, disastrous path.

Late on that decisive afternoon, he was sitting in his office reading over his latest copy of the *Supreme Court's Advance Reports*. The crook-necked lamp on his desk was on, and pooled the light in a greenish cone that glistened back from the pages of the *Report*, and profiled the hard-cut strength of his features. His eyes smarted from the fine print, and he had one hand up shading them. He was thin with high, square-set shoulders, and even in repose he gave a greyhoundish effect of restless, hard-driving energy, of unquenchable and impatient ambition.

Cora Sue Daniels opened the door softly and peeked at him around its edge. She was wearing a hat that looked like an exaggerated felt stocking cap.

"Hello, dear. Plunk said you were alone."

Daniels marked his place with a forefinger and looked up. "Hello, Cora Sue. Come in."

She crossed the office, leaned over the desk and kissed him, brushing his forehead with lips that were soft and cool and possessive. Daniels raised his hand and dabbed automatically at the spot. He had learned from experience that his wife's lips were likely to leave an indelible red mark on anything they touched.

Cora Sue twisted the neck of the lamp until it reflected on her slim, small person like a spotlight. "This is my new coat, Jim. Isn't it sweet?"

Jim winced at the choice of the adjective and watched her obediently as she twirled slowly around, holding the coat away from her and then close to her body, and then posing with a mannequin's occupational hauteur, her head tilted back.

"It's nice," Daniels said absently.

His adjective wasn't good either. Nice... The furs were deep and rich and gleaming, perfectly matched, perfectly shaded. Daniels was reflecting that it probably cost just about twice as much as he had made in the last year. But that wasn't his affair. He didn't have to pay for it.

Cora Sue's father, A.J. Bancroft, had settled a ten-million-dollar trust fund on her when she was eighteen. The income from the trust was irrevocably and completely hers.

Daniels didn't take to the idea. That and the other hundred odd million that A.J. Bancroft could shake out of his sleeve if the occasion demanded had come very close to preventing the marriage of Daniels and Cora Sue. Daniels was no fool. He liked money just as well as anyone else. But he knew that when a hundred odd million is concentrated in one fortune it ceases to be merely money. It attains a new identity. It becomes a responsibility, and a very great one. Such a responsibility, in fact, that the sheer mass of it is liable to dwarf and absorb the personality of anyone closely connected with it.

That was what Daniels didn't want. He had a fierce ambition to carve out his own career. He didn't want any of Cora Sue's money or any of A.J.'s either. He wasn't interested in the mere accumulation of money. He wanted to excel in his own profession on his own merits. He was sure that he could.

But Cora Sue had the trust fund. It couldn't be revoked. She couldn't give it away if she wanted to. Daniels was not selfish enough to want her to deny herself the benefits of the income. Nevertheless it made his own attainments seem pretty unimportant, and sometimes that annoyed him. It did now.

HE WAS FROWNING, and Cora Sue said: "Don't scowl so, dear. I think you've been straining your eyes lately. You need glasses."

"No," said Daniels. "My eyes are just tired."

Cora Sue nodded. "They are. And so are you." She watched him thoughtfully, chewing on her under-lip. "Jim...."

"What?" Daniels asked, bracing himself mentally. He recognized the signs.

"You *have* been awfully tired and nervous lately..." She took a deep breath and came out with it. "Why don't we go on a nice vacation, so you can rest?"

"Vacation?" Daniels repeated blankly. "At this time of the year?"

"Yes! *Because* it's this time of the year. Because it has been a nasty winter, and still is. Just look at the weather."

Daniels glanced reluctantly toward the window of the office. The pane reflected the green desk-light; and beyond it the wind howled in slow, mournful cadence, tapping and prying with myriad fingers that were half sleet, half snow. The whole city was cold, smoky, snowy chaos.

"And you can't get an injunction against that," Cora Sue said, waving a hand toward the window.

"Yes, I know," Daniels admitted. "But I can't go on a vacation now."

"Why not?"

"Because the courts are in session. This is the busiest time of the year for them—and for me."

"You don't have any customers—oh, all right: clients— right now, and Plunk said you didn't have any cases sched- uled for trial for the next couple of weeks."

Daniels' lips tightened. "I don't have now—no. But I will have."

"Jim, you *need* a vacation."

"Where would we go on a vacation at this time of the year?" Daniels demanded, exasperated.

"To California."

Daniels stared at her incredulously. "California!"

Cora Sue nodded. "Yes. Blair Wiles has invited us to visit him. He has places both at Phantom Lake and Desert Sands. You see, first we could go to Phantom Lake for the winter sports and then go down to Desert Sands and bake the cold out of us and swim and lie in the sun...."

Daniels was watching her narrowly. "Who is this Blair Wiles?"

The white thing that should have been a face peered in for a moment, then vanished.

Cora Sue shrugged casually. "Oh, he's an old friend of the family. Owns a shipping line, or something." Cora Sue made the shipping line sound like an aunt's old bedjacket.

"You mean the Wiles Freight Line?"

"Yes. He inherited it. He doesn't run it himself. He just sits and collects dividends."

"Nice," Daniels commented. "The answer is still no."

"But Jim! We could fly, and you wouldn't be gone long, and it wouldn't cost much! I could pay...."

"No," said Daniels.

"Please, Jim! I've already written Blair and told him that we'd come."

"Then write him again and tell him we're not."

"Jim, I haven't seen Blair for years and years, and I...."

"No," said Daniels. He kept his voice even and low with the effort he would have used on a feeble-minded, tongue-tied witness. "Now will you please go away? I'm trying to work." He reached out his hand for her.

Cora Sue stood still for a moment, staring at him. Her blue eyes were tearful, and her lower lip poked out in a childish pout. Daniels stared steadily back at her. He let his hand fall, though.

Cora Sue swallowed with a gulp. "All right, Jim. I—I'm sorry I bothered you. Goodbye."

"Goodbye," Daniels said stonily, and felt like a heel.

SHE CLOSED THE door very softly behind her. Daniels blew out his breath and immediately began a mental inventory of his idiocy. It was very thorough. The trouble was Cora Sue was right. He *did* need a vacation. His nerves were as jagged as the teeth of a saw.

But he couldn't take one now. Figured from the angle of court business, this was his most important season. And for the first time in his career he was beginning to feel that his practice was no longer a series of loose and casual threads that had no connection with each other. It was beginning to have a form and personality, a pattern. It was going to go on now, growing. He had to be here, watching and guiding it, nursing it along until it got to the point where he could sit back, like the parent of a grown son, and let it support him. He *couldn't* take a vacation. His conscience would allow him no rest even if he did.

The door opened, and Plunk Nelson said: "Hi, boss," in a falsely cheerful voice.

Plunk was short and squat and ugly. He had a thick-lipped mouth, and he wore enormous horn-rimmed spectacles that gave him the vaguely stupid air of a frog trying to read a book. He was Daniels' secretary, receptionist, assistant, and general major-domo. He was determined to become an orchestra leader. He was holding his job temporarily, until such time as Fame and Fortune came along and tapped him on the shoulder. This made a pleasantly restful legend, and gave him a coat of protective coloration.

Daniels said: "By any chance, do you remember my telling you not to give out information about my clients or my cases?"

Plunk blinked. "Well, Jim, she's your wife…"

"Never mind who it is. Don't do it."

Plunk shook his head vigorously. "I won't again. Honest. But, Jim, you really ought to take a vacation…."

Daniels didn't say anything. But his look was so eloquently murderous that Plunk shivered and backed out of the office and shut the door hurriedly.

Daniels sighed. He covered his eyes with the palms of his hands, bracing his elbows on the desk. He breathed evenly and slowly, trying to fight down the quivery jumping rawness of his nerves.

He was still sitting that way when Plunk opened the door again. Daniels looked up at him.

"A customer." Plunk's eyes were glistening eagerly behind the thick lenses of his glasses. "A dame. And guess who?"

"I don't feel like guessing games," Daniels said savagely. "Who?"

"Mrs. Gordon Gregory!" Plunk said triumphantly.

"Who's she?" Daniels demanded.

"The babe with the production-belt husbands!"

"That what?" Daniels asked blankly.

Plunk spread his hands. "Don't you ever read the scandal sheets, Jim?"

"Not if I can help it."

"Well, look," said Plunk. "Mrs. Gregory is the widow of the Gregory that owned all them steel mills. He married her when he was about eighty-two because he said she had such a cheerful smile—ha-ha!—and he left her all his dough when he died on account he was an orphan and didn't have no kids. She's got so much she can't count it."

"What about the husbands?" Daniels asked.

"She's been married about six times since then, is all. Every one of 'em took her for a ride, and she had to settle plenty on 'em to get rid of 'em. On top of that she's been sued about ninety times by other guys for breach of promise and by dames that claimed she alienated their husbands' affections. If you could land her business, Jim! Boy! She's *always* knockin' around in court for one reason or another!"

Daniels nodded slowly. "Send her in."

"Come to think of it," Plunk said dreamily, "maybe I ought to shine up to her. Maybe she'd put up some dough for me to organize a band with. I got just the arrangements and the boys to step right into some big broadcasting spot and wow 'em. I can see the bunch now—all with monkey jackets and white pants with gold braid down the seams— settin' there and ridin' out a tune while I wave the stick and give the crowd the old personality—"

"Send—Mrs.—Gregory—in!"

Plunk came out of it. "Uh? Oh. Sure, sure. Right away, Jim."

MRS. GREGORY WAS utterly different from what Daniels had expected after Plunk's categorical buildup. She was small, rather plain, and she *did* have a nice smile. It was a pleasant, wistful, appealing smile, childlike and trusting and timid. It begged people not to be too outrageous. She wore a fur coat that made Daniels think of Cora Sue's multiplied by two. She had brownish, straight hair and a round, plain face that was innocent of any makeup. She wore three diamond rings on one hand and four on the other, and any of the stones could have been used as a naval base.

Daniels blinked; his eyes hurt. Mrs. Gregory's hands could have illuminated a Hollywood opening. Plunk pulled up a chair, bowed Mrs. Gregory into it with penguin grace and tiptoed out of the room.

Mrs. Gregory noticed Daniels' eyes riveted helplessly on the diamonds, and she held up her hands and wiggled her stubby fingers.

"I like diamond rings," said Mrs. Gregory, smiling. "Don't you?"

"Well—yes," Daniels admitted. He liked the Fourth of July, too.

"I've always liked them," said Mrs. Gregory, admiring the rings. She looked over them at Daniels. "You're Cora Sue Bancroft's husband, aren't you?"

"Cora Sue *Daniels* is my wife," Daniels said shortly.

"Of course. That's what I meant. I've heard ever so much about you. How clever and brilliant—and honest you are."

"Well, thank you," Daniels said, embarrassed. "You—you wished to see me about some business?"

"Oh, yes! This is very, very confidential."

"Is it?" Daniels asked impassively.

"Yes. Very. Now I want to ask you a question, Mr. Daniels. Is it—is it possible for a lawyer like you to go with a client to transact some business. To—to protect her?"

"Surely," said Daniels.

Mrs. Gregory nodded, relieved. "That's fine. This business of mine is quite a ways away. It will take you several days."

Daniels held up his hand. "Just a moment, then. You understand that if I have to leave my office for any length of time, it will mean neglecting any other clients that might want my services. In other words, it will cost you quite a lot, depending on just how long I'm away."

Mrs. Gregory's hand made a glittering, casual sweep in the air. "Oh, that's all right! The cost doesn't matter. This is very important."

"I see. Where am I to go with you?"

"To California."

Daniels blinked. "You said—California?"

"Yes. At Phantom Lake."

"Oh," said Daniels slowly. "You wouldn't, by any chance, be planning on staying at a place owned by a man named Blair Wiles, would you?"

"Why, yes! Aren't you clever though? Blair invited me to come and stay, and I'm sure he wouldn't mind if I brought my attorney along—"

Daniels stood up. "But *I'd* mind. I'm sorry, Mrs. Gregory. I can't handle your business for you."

She stared up at him. "Why not?"

Daniels shook his head. "I don't wish to discuss the matter further. I can't handle it. Doubtless you can find another attorney who will be glad to. Good day."

Mrs. Gregory protested helplessly. "But—but you must! I don't know any other attorney who can be trusted—that I'd want to trust with—with—"

Daniels went over and opened the door "I'm sorry. I can't serve you in this. Good day."

"But there's no one else—" Mrs. Gregory wailed.

Daniels moved the door meaningly. "Good day, Mrs. Gregory."

She went to it slowly, still protesting vaguely, like a bewildered child. Daniels went back to his desk. He was so angry he couldn't control the trembling of his hands.

PLUNK APPEARED IN the doorway, his face twisted up into a weirdly dismayed grimace. "Jim! Jim, what—what—"

"Shut up and get out!"

"Huh? Oh. Sure. Sure, sure, Jim."

Daniels picked up the telephone on his desk and dialed savagely. He waited in a fever of darkly bitter rage, and a polite smoothly southern voice said:

"This here is the residence of Mr. James Daniels."

"Call Mrs. Daniels."

"Yes, sah, Mr. Daniels. Hold the phone."

Cora Sue's voice said cheerfully: "Hello, Jim, dear."

Daniels' words came in a sudden harsh rush: "Listen, Cora Sue. I told you that I am *not* going to take a vacation! I meant that! I am not going to go to California! And I don't like the idea of your sending your friends up here and trying to bribe me into going with fake cases and charity fees! I will not have you interfering with my business with tricks like that! Is that clear?"

"But, Jim! Wait! I—I don't know what—"

"I'm not going to argue about it! But don't ever do it again!"

He slammed the telephone back in its cradle and sat down in his chair. He was breathing as though he had just finished the ascent of Everest and now he felt a queer, let-down sickness deep inside him. He had let his temper get completely away from him.

Plunk opened the door again, cautiously. "Jim...."

"What?" Daniels asked wearily.

"Listen. When Mrs. Gregory went into your office, she left her handbag on a chair in here. It's set with diamonds and stuff, and I didn't want it lyin' around loose like that, so I picked it up and put it in the desk. But it opened when I took it out again to give it to her just now as she was leaving, and there was a gun in it!"

Daniels shrugged. "Well, what of it? She has the right to carry a gun if she wishes. Was it set with diamonds?"

Plunk shook his head slowly. "That's it. I wouldn't have thought nothin' of it if it had been one of them funny little pearl handled babies women carry when they think they gotta have protection or somethin'. This here one wasn't. This one was a .38 Smith and Wesson Special. It filled that whole bag full. That ain't no ladies' toy, Jim. That gun packs a mean punch."

"Forget it, Plunk," Daniels said. "I'm not interested in Mrs. Gregory and her armament. She can string a Howitzer around her neck for all of me."

Plunk squinted, worried. "I dunno now, Jim. A woman wouldn't go carryin' a whoppin' big revolver like that around with her unless she had a mighty good reason for doin' it. That thing must weigh two and a half pounds. You suppose she's plannin' on takin' a pop at somebody?"

"I wouldn't know," Daniels said with magnificent finality. "Mrs. Gregory and her possible course of action don't interest me in the slightest."

Later, he was to think of those words often.

2

THE LAWYER TAKES A TRIP

IT WAS DARK when Daniels drove down the wide, tree-lined street. The wind had stiffened, and the snow came down in a long, fierce slant, plastering itself endlessly against the little coupé's windshield. The windshield wiper groaned and clicked and muttered, fighting unavailingly to keep its measured pace.

Daniels swung wide into the middle of the street, chains banging under the fenders, turned up into a wide, graveled driveway. He went through an open iron gate, past the thick hedge beyond it, and the great, high, white length of the house was ahead of him.

Daniels winced mentally every time he saw the house. That was foolish, too, and he admitted it. It wasn't his house. It was Cora Sue's.

Cora Sue had seen it at one time or another and liked it. When she had gotten married she had called up the trust company and told them so. That was all there was to it. When Cora Sue and Daniels returned home from their honeymoon, the house was all ready for them—bought and paid for, furnished by the city's most exclusive and expensive interior decorator, staffed with a complete set of properly wooden-jawed servants.

The trust company was efficient. No doubt about that. Daniels often thought they were a little too efficient. They ran the place. They hired, fired, and paid all the servants— except Poinsetta, Cora Sue's personal maid. They paid all the bills. Daniels never even saw any of them. Not that the trust company officials ever intruded. They were as unobtrusive as the plumbing. Daniels had never seen any of them, either. But they were always present in spirit. Daniels felt like the favored guest of a palatial hotel.

Stopping in front of the wide front entrance, he put these thoughts resolutely out of his mind. Those things, and a good many others, were annoying, but they weren't Cora Sue's fault. They were the fault of the fact that she had been born with a lot of money. She couldn't be blamed for that any more than Daniels could be blamed for the fact that he was born with a strawberry mark on his left breast. Daniels had let his temper slip once today, and he was determined not to let it happen again. He was already feeling pretty contrite about the way he had spoken to Cora Sue over the telephone.

His footsteps sounded hollow and cold going across the porch, and then the big front door swung back and bathed him in warm, soft light.

"Evenin', Mr. Daniels!" Poinsetta greeted. She was fat and short and very black. She had been Cora Sue's nurse ever since Cora Sue's mother had died, and she was an established and respected member of the household. She took no back talk from any of the "company trash" as she called the servants installed by the trust company, and next to Cora Sue, Daniels was the apple of her eye.

"Hello, Poinsetta," Daniels said.

A uniformed butler came in through the door to the servant's quarters and advanced with a measured, stately tread.

Poinsetta eyed him evilly. "Git!"

The butler stopped short. He blinked at Poinsetta warily and then beat a dignified retreat.

"Huh!" said Poinsetta triumphantly. She helped Daniels out of his coat, shook the snow out of it carefully, hung it up. "Mighty nasty weather, Mr. Daniels."

Daniels nodded absently. "Yes. Where's Cora Sue?"

Poinsetta opened her mouth vaguely. "Huh?"

"Cora Sue. Where is she?"

"Why—why, she gone."

"Gone!" Daniels echoed incredulously. "Gone where?"

"Californy."

DANIELS SWALLOWED. HE felt as lost and forlorn as if he had suddenly been dropped in the middle of a strange desert. His breath seemed to have caught in a hot, tight ball in his throat, and he had to swallow and then swallow again before he could speak.

"When—wher...."

"She start goin' right after you call on the phone."

"Oh," Daniels said weakly. "Why—why didn't you go with her?"

"She say somebody got to stay home and take care of you because you ain't fit for to take care of yourself. And anyway, I got to watch this here company trash. They go to stealin' everything that ain't nailed down if I don't watch 'em."

"Oh," said Daniels.

Poinsetta watched him sympathetically. "You and Cora Sue, you got yourselves a mad on, huh?"

Daniels nodded slowly. "I guess so, Poinsetta."

"Cora Sue, she cry after you talk to her on the phone. She cry when she go, too."

Daniels stared silently and miserably at the floor.

Poinsetta said slowly: "Mr. Daniels, she ain't done what you said she done."

Daniels jerked his head around. "What?"

He stared at her.

"She ain't done what you bawled her out for."

"How do you know?" Daniels demanded tensely.

"She say so to me. She say you bawl her out for sendin' you fake cases. She say she don't know what you talkin' about, she ain't never done that, at all."

"Are you sure?" Daniels demanded, horrified.

Poinsetta nodded firmly. "I sure. Cora Sue, she don't never lie to Poinsetta. Never, besides, she ain't gonna monkey with that business of yours. No, sir! She scared to death of that business. She tell me lots of times that business mean an awful lot to you, and she goin' to keep out of it and never bother you. She say when you get mad about that business, you can sure raise hell."

"I did this time, all right," Daniels admitted, staring blankly ahead of him. "I was sure she sent Mrs. Gregory with some crazy idea of fooling me into going to California. It was too much of a coincidence—Mrs. Gregory coming in right after Cora Sue had been talking about going to the same place, wanting to pay me to go there… Good Lord! Now I have done it! Losing my temper and giving her the devil for something she didn't even do. Was—was she mad, Poinsetta?"

"No," said Poinsetta judiciously. "She just cryin'. But she

gonna be mad—awful mad—pretty soon. That's the way she goes. First she cries, and then she gets mad."

"She's got a right to be this time," Daniels said. He drew a deep breath, throwing his shoulders back. "Poinsetta! I'm going to California—now!"

Poinsetta grinned. "Yo' all packed." She waddled toward the stairs, stopped at the bottom to look back over one shoulder. "She goin' by the airplane."

Daniels nodded. He went into the study, took the telephone directory out of its carved mahogany cabinet, flipped through the pages until he found the number he wanted. He dialed it with quick, savage haste and waited impatiently.

A polite feminine voice said: "Northwest Air Lines."

Daniels said: "I want to reserve a passage to California on the night plane."

"I'm sorry, sir. All passenger planes are grounded on account of the storm."

"Grounded!" Daniels said blankly.

"Yes, sir. The last plane went out at four-thirty this afternoon."

That was the plane Cora Sue must have taken, and Daniels chewed his lip in indecision.

The polite voice said: "If you wish, sir, you can reserve passage on the morning plane at Salt City. That is out of the storm area. You can make connections by taking the train there tonight."

"All right," said Daniels. "Make that reservation for me. The name is James A. Daniels."

"Thank you, sir."

Daniels hung up and flipped through the directory

again until he found the number of the railroad station. He dialed it, and when a voice answered, asked:

"What time does the Western Limited stop here tonight?"

"At seven-twelve, sir."

"Thanks," Daniels said. He looked at his watch. He had about a half hour to pack and drive ten miles through traffic across the city. He dropped the telephone back in its cradle and ran out into the hall.

"Poinsetta! Poinsetta! Hurry! My bag, quick."

"I hurryin', Mr. Daniels. Don't fret me."

3

THE PRINCE TAKES DINNER

DANIELS MADE IT—BY one sandy eyebrow. The train was moving by the time he got arranged in his seat. The Limited was a new, fast train, and it started without any rumbling or banging or jerking. It slid away into the night like a great, quiet beast, and the only noticeable noise was the slight click-click, click-click of its wheels over switches. It gathered speed imperceptibly, and scattered lights began to flick past like steaming yellow blurs.

Daniels leaned back into the cushioned softness of his seat and breathed evenly and deeply, trying to stifle the pounding thunder of his heart. This was the last car in the train, an extra, and there were only a few passengers in it.

Daniels looked them over casually, not very interested until he happened to notice the man across the aisle. He smiled sympathetically, then. The man was young, so young he could hardly be called a man. At the moment, he looked more like a boy because he was sleeping.

His thin face was wan and wearily relaxed. He was curled up in his seat, and his slight body swayed back and forth with the slight motion of the train. He was wearing a wrinkled, shiny blue suit that didn't fit very well. His hair was thick and brown and stubborn, sticking out straight in a clump at the back of his head.

Watching him, Daniels wondered what he was doing on a special-fare train like this one. The suit had the two-years-ago look of a hand-me-down, and its wearer didn't look exactly overnourished. His cheeks were pinched and pale; and his body was scrawny.

The train went around a curve, and the boy swayed loosely outward away from the seat. Daniels thought surely he was going to fall off, and he stiffened, preparing to call a warning. But the youth didn't fall. Something held him by the left arm. Something that clicked a little.

The youth's left arm was covered by an overcoat, but the movement of his body had shifted the coat slightly, and Daniels caught a glimpse of bright metal under it. Daniels blew out his pent-up breath in a noiseless whistle. The youth's left wrist was handcuffed to the arm of his seat.

ANOTHER MAN CAME down the aisle and stopped beside the youth's seat. He was heavy-set, but he walked quickly and lightly for all of that. He wore dark clothes and a broad-brimmed black hat tilted casually on the back of his head. His face was broad and heavy-jowled, shot with tiny red veins, and his eyes were small and alert and suspicious staring at Daniels.

"Hello," Daniels said.

The heavy-set man's eyes didn't move or blink. "Hello," he said finally. He turned away then and took a couple of candy bars out of his pocket. He leaned over and touched the youth's thin shoulder. "Pete. Pete, wake up."

The youth slept on, drugged with weariness too old for his years and experience.

"Pete," said the heavy-set man again. His voice was surprisingly gentle. "Come on, Pete. Wake up."

The youth didn't move, and the heavy cadence of his breathing went on unchanged. He was occupying all of the seat, and the heavy-set man stood uncertainly in the aisle, staring down at him.

Daniels said: "You can sit over here if you want to."

The heavy-set man glanced at him sharply again. He was silent for a moment, studying Daniels, and then he nodded and said:

"Thanks."

Daniels moved over, and the heavy-set man sat down beside him.

"Hate to wake him up," said the heavy-set man. He looked tired, too, now that he was relaxed. He took off his hat and wiped a flushed forehead with his handkerchief. "The kid ain't slept for two days. And besides, when he's sleeping he gets a chance to forget…."

"What?" Daniels asked.

"Things," said the heavy-set man.

Daniels was curious. "My name is Daniels. I'm an attorney." He took one of his cards from his wallet, extended it.

The heavy-set man looked at it thoughtfully. "Glad to know you. I'm Biggers—deputy-sheriff from Crater County, California."

"What did he do?" Daniels asked, nodding across the aisle. "Escape from the reform school?"

Biggers shook his head slowly. "No. I sure wish that was all he had done. He murdered his gal."

"Murdered!" Daniels echoed incredulously. "That kid?"

"Yeah. Pete Carson is his name. We had him in jail

waitin' for his trial, and he lammed out on us. Got picked up back East on a vag charge, and they recognized him from our circulars. I'm bringin' him back."

"But he's so young!"

"Don't I know it?" Biggers asked gloomily. "Listen, I've known that kid for years. He's always been a good kid, and I've always liked him. What do you think I feel like—draggin' him back to what he's goin' to?"

"What is he going to?"

Biggers made a mute and eloquent circle around his neck with his forefinger and thumb.

"No!" said Daniels, sickened at the thought.

BIGGERS NODDED WEARILY. "Only they don't hang 'em in California now. They put 'em in a gas chamber. But that ain't so pleasant to think about, either."

Daniels protested: "But if he hasn't been tried yet...."

Biggers shook his head. "It's one of them things. It's an open-and-shut case. It's on ice. Pete ain't got any defense at all, and this escape of his ain't gonna do him any good. I don't have to testify at his trial, thank God for that. This here is bad enough without that, too."

"Where did the murder take place?" Daniels asked.

"At the upper end of Crater County. That's the Phantom Lake district."

"Phantom Lake," Daniels repeated. That name was beginning to haunt him. It was like the refrain in a song you don't like that is played too often on the radio. First Cora Sue, and then Mrs. Gregory, and now a murderer. He looked up at Biggers. "Do you happen to know a man by the name of Blair Wiles?"

"Him? Sure." Biggers' eyes were alert and curious. "Friend of yours?"

"No. I never saw him in my life. I've heard about him, though, lots of times."

"Uh," said Biggers. He shrugged heavily. "Well, it just goes to show you."

"Show you what?"

"He killed a guy, but he's still runnin' around loose. He throws a bit more weight than Pete does."

Daniels stared incredulously. "Wiles... killed a man?"

"Yeah. It went down as an accident, and maybe—if you ain't too particular—that's what it was."

"How did it happen?" Daniels asked.

"Wiles was a lush. He had a handyman and stooge he took around with him to drive for him when he was too drunk. Name of Randall. Well, this time Wiles got drunk but he wouldn't let Randall drive home. They were up on that Phantom Lake road, and that ain't no place to get comical with a car. There's a lot of curves, and Wiles went off one of 'em. The car dropped a hundred feet into a canyon and burned. Killed Randall."

"Was Wiles hurt?"

"Plenty. Spent two years in a hospital. Nobody could figure out how he got even that much alive. I guess maybe you could say he paid for his little trick that way."

A dining-car waiter in a white jacket came through the car tapping his musical chimes softly.

"Dinnah. Last call for dinnah. Last call."

Biggers got up. "I'll have to wake Pete up now. He ain't been eatin' at all lately."

He took the handcuffs off Pete Carson's lax, bony wrist.

He straightened the thin body up on the seat and shook him back and forth gently.

"Pete! Come on, now! Wake up!"

"Huh? What?"

"Wake up, boy."

"Huh? Oh." He dug wearily at his eyes with his knuckles. "What, Mr. Biggers?"

"We gotta eat, Pete."

"I—I don't think I want nothin' to eat, Mr. Biggers. I don't—feel like eatin'. You lock me up and go ahead. I'll stay here."

Biggers shook his head. "No, Pete. Come along now and eat something. Just for a favor to me."

Pete got up reluctantly. "All right, Mr. Biggers. I—I'll try, anyway."

"That's the boy. You come on now and wash up, and then you'll feel better. You gotta eat something once in awhile."

"Why?" Pete asked wearily.

Biggers cleared his throat uncomfortably. "Come on, Pete. Let's wash up."

THEY WENT ON down the aisle, and Daniels watched them go, his face twisted in instinctive aversion. It was Daniels' inherent sympathy for the underdog in his struggles with the merciless mill of the Law that had spurred him on to becoming an attorney. He had never lost that tilt-at-the-windmill feeling. He had it now, for Pete Carson, stronger than he had ever had it before.

He wanted to help, and he was wondering if there wasn't some way he could when he noticed the man standing quietly in the aisle beside his seat.

"Mr. Daniels?" the man asked. "Mr. James A. Daniels?"

Daniels nodded. "Yes." He stared curiously at the man. He hadn't noticed him in the car before. He was to learn later that this was only natural. Hassan had a gift for receding quietly into his background that would have taught a cheetah tricks in stealth.

"I am Prince Dak Hassan," he said, with a bow as faint as his accent. "I am very pleased indeed to make your acquaintance."

He made a quick sharp click of his heels. He was short and slender man with graceful, catlike movements. He wore expensive gray tweeds, dark blue shirt, a darker blue tie. His face was a perfectly smooth, round, darkly tanned oval, and his eyes were cool, round green. He had an ingratiating smile and perfect, glistering teeth.

"How do you do?" Daniels said blankly.

Dak Hassan bowed again and sat down beside Daniels without being asked. That was also characteristic.

"You do not know me? You have not read my name in the papers?"

"No," Daniels answered truthfully.

Dak Hassan shrugged gracefully. "It seems hardly possible. It is often there. In the society columns."

"I never read them," said Daniels.

"No?" Dak Hassan was surprised. "That is very strange—in your case."

"What do you mean—in my case?"

Dak Hassan smiled. "I cannot have made a mistake. You married Cora Sue Bancroft, did you not?"

Daniels' voice congealed slightly. "Yes."

Dak Hassan spread his hands. "So that is why I am surprised."

Daniels frowned. "I'm sorry. I'm a little tired tonight, and I don't seem to be following you very well. Let's start over again. You said you were a prince?"

"Indeed, yes."

"Of what?"

"Radisztan."

Daniels blinked. "What did you say?"

"Radisztan. It was a province of the old Russian Empire."

"Oh," said Daniels.

"It is a very old title," Dak Hassan said modestly. "Mine is a very ancient and honorable family. Indeed, yes."

"Oh," Daniels said again.

"Is yours?" Dak Hassan asked.

"No," Daniels admitted.

"You have no social position?"

"Not a bit."

"How strange," said Dak Hassan. "How very, very strange. But that makes your accomplishment all the more of a credit to you."

Daniels was watching him narrowly. "Just what accomplishment are you talking about?"

"Marrying the Bancroft money, of course. What else?"

"Marrying the Bancroft…" Daniels' voice trailed off, and his lips tightened.

Dak Hassan nodded amiably. "Yes. Of course."

Daniels started to get up. His fists were itching.

"Please," said Dak Hassan smoothly. "Engaging in fisticuffs is not only rude and undignified but in this case, quite unnecessary. We are in the same business, you and I."

Daniels stared at him. He still was sure he'd better not try to speak.

"Yes. Quite so. One must have money. If one is not lucky enough to be born with it and is not stupid enough to wish to work for it, then one must marry it."

Daniels stood up. "I think I've heard enough." His tone was ever and as full of menace as a red light.

"Please," said Dak Hassan pleasantly, "Calm yourself."

Daniels reached for him and stopped with his hand an inch from Dak Hassan's expensively tailored shoulder. Dak Hassan hadn't made any noticeable movement, but he was holding a gun in his right hand.

HE HELD IT down low, out of sight of any of the passengers in front or in back of them. It was a .25-caliber Mauser automatic—a wicked, efficient-looking little gun. Dak Hassan held it as though he knew how to use it.

"Please sit down," said Dak Hassan in his smooth, pleasant voice. "If one is of royal lineage, one must take precautions against being rudely handled. Please do sit down. If you attack me, I will shoot. I assure you of that."

He *would* shoot. Daniels knew it suddenly. Dak Hassan's eyes were as cold as greenish marbles, and his pupils looked like tiny, dead-black pinpoints, Daniels sat down slowly.

"Thank you," said Dak Hassan. He put the small automatic back into the inner pocket of his vest. His expression was as pleasant as ever. "You Americans are so sentimental about marriage, I have noted. One must take precautions when speaking to the ordinary person, but I do not think it necessary in your case."

Daniels found a perverse humor in the situation all at once, and he grinned, darkly amused.

"Thank you," said Dak Hassan. "That is so much better.

I am an admirer of yours. It would be most unfortunate if we should quarrel over a triviality."

Daniels nodded. "It would. So you're in the business of marrying money?"

"Oh, yes. Quite so."

"How are you doing?"

Dak Hassan shrugged. "Indifferently well at present. I shall do much better shortly."

"So?" Daniels said. "How?"

"I am going to marry Mrs. Gordon Gregory."

"You know her?"

"Faintly," said Daniels.

"She does not, unfortunately, have as much money as your father-in-law does, but she has enough, I think, to support me in a manner befitting my position." He spoke of it as if it was something he had skillfully run-up out of a few bits of wire.

"Oh, undoubtedly," said Daniels. "Does she know you're going to marry her?"

"She is not, as yet, irresistibly convinced of that fact. But she soon will be, I assure you."

"I see."

"And then, there is my title, of course."

"Certainly," said Daniels. "Your title."

"She will marry me," Dak Hassan said with quiet confidence. "I do not anticipate any great difficulties, although at the moment she is trying to elude me under the mistaken impression that if I am not near her she will be able to forget me." He paused, quietly amused. "No woman can forget Prince Dak Hassan."

"I don't doubt it," Daniels commented.

"Thank you. I am following her now to persuade her of that obvious fact."

"Following her?" Daniels repeated.

"Yes. She is going to Phantom Lake. So am I."

"Oh," said Daniels. "You, too." His mental radio tuned on again on that grinding refrain.

Dak Hassan raised his eye-brows. "Why do you speak in that tone?"

"My wife is there."

Dak Hassan spread his hands. "I understand. You are apprehensive because I might displace you in her affections? Have no fear. When one is a gentleman, one does not poach on another's preserves."

"That relieves my mind."

"It is nothing, my friend. If one cannot trust a prince of royal lineage, whom can one trust?"

"I sometimes wonder," Daniels said. "I'm a little hungry. Will you join me at dinner?"

"Indeed, yes! It will be a very great pleasure. You will pay for it, of course?"

"Oh, of course," said Daniels.

4

THE KID TAKES A CHANCE

IT WAS MORNING, and the sun was warm and incredibly bright when Daniels got out of his taxi at the intersection and paid off the driver. He waited at the corner until the signal clanged and then burred comfortably to itself, changing its mechanical arms from "Go" to "Stop". Then he walked across the street and down.

His overcoat was hot and thick over his arm, and the handles of his heavy suitcase were wet and sweaty in his palm. The sun pierced the back of his suit and made an uncomfortably warm spot between his shoulder blades. Several pedestrians glanced curiously and knowingly at the overcoat as he walked along.

He turned in a lot between two buildings, walked under a sign that said: *Cars for Rent—U-Drive,* in enormous block-red letters. A board shack stood on the corner of the lot, and there was a fat man sitting on an old auto seat in front of it, lounging back comfortably and smoking a big, black cigar.

"Howdy," he greeted, moving the cigar so he could talk around it. He sized up Daniels' suit and overcoat and grinned. "Just come in from the East?"

"Yes," Daniels admitted.

"You're smart, comin' here," the fat man informed him enthusiastically. "Ain't this the most marvelous country you ever laid eyes on? Take a look across the street. You see that lawn over there? It's green, ain't it? You see that tree in front? It's green, too. And feel that sun!" If he had been directly responsible for the climate he could not have been smugger.

"I am feeling it," Daniels said.

"It's wonderful! And this is in the dead of winter, mind you! Why, I was just readin' in the paper that they're havin' a blizzard back East! Can you imagine that? Think of them saps back there diggin' out of the snow, freezin' their ears and gettin' chilblains, and here I sit without even a coat on! And, look! You see that tree down on the corner? That's a palm tree. A real, live palm tree! I bet you never seen one of them before, did you?"

"Yes," said Daniels, wondering if the palm tree were some relation of the fat man's.

"Where?" the fat man demanded skeptically.

"In California. I went to college here."

"You did? Where?"

"Stanford."

The fat man thought a minute. "Stanford. Oh, yeah. That's the school up north we always beat at football. You shoulda gone down here. We got lots better colleges down here."

"I'll remember that next time," Daniels told him.

"Yeah," said the fat man. "Stanford's in northern California and that's just sort of the hind-end of California. That part of the state don't amount to much."

"What do the people in northern California think about that?"

The fat man shrugged. "Them? Who cares? They're crazy or they wouldn't live there. Take San Francisco—that's an awful place. They got nothing but fog there—day and night, winter and summer. It's terrible!"

"Ever been there?" Daniels asked.

"No! And I ain't goin' there, neither. You want to buy you a nice second-hand car, mister? That's the thing to do. Then you can drive around and see the scenery. Why, you can go down south of here—few miles and pick ripe oranges right off the trees, right now, and…."

"I don't want to buy a car. I want to rent one."

"Oh," said the fat man. "For how long?"

"About a week."

"Okay. Where you goin'?"

"Up above Phantom Lake."

The fat man pursed his lips and shook his head. "You don't wanta go up there. It's 'way up in the mountains. It's cold up there, mister. You can see the snow on top from here." The fat man had obviously been delegated by a resourceful providence to keep Jim from folly.

"I still want to go there."

"Okay," said the fat man resignedly. "Okay. But are you sure you can get through? It snowed up there last night."

"Yes. I called up. They said the roads were passable."

"Ummm," said the fat man. "Well, I'll tell you now, mister. We got the best roads in the world out here, and we got the best highway service, too, but sometimes the boys get a little optimistic. When they say passable they might mean the roads are passable if you got a snow plow with you."

"I'll take a chance."

"Okay. Damn, now I got to find you some chains. You'll need 'em up there. I don't know whether I got any or not. They don't equip cars with 'em in this country any more. Never need 'em. Wait while I look."

THE ROAD HAD been climbing for hours—climbing in long, gracefully banked curves that went on endlessly upward. Daniels' hired sedan burbled and grunted and knocked protestingly, and his arms were beginning to ache from constantly turning the steering wheel back and forth, back and forth.

The air was colder, much colder, and it had a heady, winy tang to it. It was light and thin and clear, and Daniels could feel his heart pumping harder to make up for its loss in oxygen content. The vegetation along the roadside was dark and resentfully shrunken with frostbite.

Occasionally as the road turned majestically back and forth, he could catch a glimpse of the valley, miles away now and down thousands of feet below, like a green-and-brown checkerboard. Nearer him, there were brown, dirty half-melted rolls of snow high on the canyon sides. Rocks were cold gray lumps sticking out of the sparse earth.

The red ball of the sun slipped down behind the mountains ahead and night dropped on him noiselessly, like the swift descent of a black curtain. Daniels switched on the lights. The road kept climbing steadily. It turned around once far enough for him to get a glimpse of the valley again. It was still day down there, bright and warm with sunlight, and then the road went away from it finally and the mountains gathered closer, cold and awesomely lonely.

The snow gathered more thickly along the roadside, glinting back icily bright from the headlights, pinching in on the edges of the road, narrowing it.

Daniels saw a service station and headed in beside the brightly painted pumps. The attendant came trotting out, his breath making a long steamy plume under the lights.

"Hi! Gettin' kind of cold, eh?"

Daniels nodded. "Pretty cold. Fill it up, will you?"

"Sure. Going up much higher?"

"Up back of Phantom Lake."

"That's topside. You'll run into plenty snow. We got a lot of it last night. If you've got chains, you'd better put 'em on here. You'll need 'em a mile or so up."

"Are the roads clear?" Daniels asked.

"I think so. The boys been workin' on 'em all day. They should be about through by now. They'll be on control when you get up high."

"On control?" Daniels questioned.

"Yeah. They only let cars go through one way at a time. No room to pass. You may have to wait for awhile if anybody's comin' the other way. They'll signal you."

Daniels put the chains on with the attendant's help, thanked him and paid him, and drove on up the endless grade. The chains beat noisily on the fenders for awhile and then the snow crept across the surface of the road and muffled their clatter. The headlights glinted in brilliant reflections from snow-burdened brush and stubby trees.

Daniels had lost all track of the time, hypnotized by the steady, labored drone of the motor, when he saw the jerking swing of an electric lantern ahead of him. He slowed up and stopped beside the man who held it.

The man came around to the side window, beating his arms across his chest to stir his circulation. He was stocky and short and young with a cheerfully red, wind-bitten face. He wore a thick blue stocking cap and a sheep-skin jacket.

"Hi, mister. Goin' up much further?"

"I'm going up to Blair Wiles' lodge."

The man nodded. "You can get through that far all right. The boys with the plow are on up above a ways. Do you know where Wiles' place is?"

"No. Never been there."

"It's about two miles on up from here. You'll see his sign on the right side of the road. Turn off there. Don't park on this road."

"Can I get through?"

"Yeah. Wiles' chauffeur was down today, and he told me he'd shoveled a way through to the garage. You can get that far. The garage is about two hundred yards above the road. Wiles' lodge is about a mile up from there. You'll have to walk. There's a path and be careful you don't get off it. The drifts are too deep for a man to get through without skis or snow-shoes, and it's going to snow some more tonight. Better hurry along."

"Thanks," Daniels said.

HE DROVE ON. The snow plow had been at work on the drifts here, and the road ran along like a narrow, curving trench with glistening white side-walls. The grade was steeper and not so well constructed. The sedan thumped and chugged along laboriously.

Daniels found the sign—an artistically jagged board with the word *Wiles* printed on it in red block letters. There was a break in the drift beside it, and Daniels turned in. Tires had chewed their way through the flat, unbroken surface of the snow, and Daniels steered along their tracks. Branches whipped coldly along the fenders, and the car rocked crazily over bumps, groaning in every joint.

The tire tracks went up a steep hump, angling slightly sideways for purchase, and Daniels' sedan quit halfway up with a final tired groan. Daniels got it into low, raced the motor, kicked out the clutch suddenly. The car edged forward, skidding slightly, made it up over the hump with a triumphant, exhausted sputter.

There was a small, cleared space here with the dark outline of a building almost covered with snow at the far side. Daniels judged that this was the garage, and he drove up against one of the doors and got out of the car. He took a long, deep breath of relief and then opened the hood of the car, intending to drain the water out of the radiator.

He was groping down into the engine, looking for the petcock, when some slight movement caught his eye. He straightened up, startled.

There was a man crouched under the dark shadow of the eaves of the garage. Daniels could see only the small dim blur of his figure, and the steely glint of some object he was holding out straight in his right hand, pointing it at Daniels.

His voice came thin and raw, shakily desperate: "Put your hands up! Quick! I'll shoot!"

Daniels stiffened and raised his hands slowly above his head.

"Stand still, now! Don't you move!"

Daniels said: "It's Pete Carson, isn't it?"

The metallic object jerked in the man's hand. "Huh? How'd you know? Who're you?"

"My name is Daniels. I sat across the aisle from you on the train the night before last. Can I put my hands down, Pete? I haven't got a gun, and I'm not going to hurt you."

"Yeah. But don't you try any tricks! I'll shoot!"

"Shoot?" Daniels questioned gently. "What with, Pete? That wrench you're pointing at me?"

Pete's breath caught in a taut sob. "Don't you come for me! I'll sling it at you! I—I will!"

"I'm not going to come for you," Daniels assured him. "I want to help you, Pete, if I can. How did you get away from Biggers?"

"He went to sleep, and I jumped out of the car and run. He didn't have the handcuffs on me. I hitched a ride on a truck and got up here."

"How did you and Biggers get to California so quickly?"

"Biggers, his nephew flies a plane—does skywriting and orchard-spraying and stuff. He was waitin' for us in Reno, and he flew us in."

"I see. Come here, Pete. I won't hurt you."

Pete came closer, step by step, warily. His face was pinched a dead, paper white by the cold, and he was shivering under his thin overcoat in spasmodic, uncontrollable jerks. His eyes were wild and dilated with panic.

Daniels watched him carefully. "I've got some brandy in my suitcase."

HE PULLED THE case out of the rear of the sedan, opened it with fingers that were stiff and clumsy inside his gloves. He found a hammered silver flask and handed it to Pete. Pete opened it and took a long, gulping swallow. He doubled up, coughing in choked, rasping gasps.

"I ain't used—ain't used…."

Daniels rescued the flask. "I know. But it will make you feel better. Had anything to eat today?"

"N—no."

"I thought not. Listen, Pete. I'm an attorney, and I want to help you. Do you believe that?"

"Why?" Pete demanded suspiciously. "What do you wanta help me for? I ain't got no money to pay you."

"I don't want to be paid. All I want is to help you. Will you believe that, Pete? Will you trust me?"

Pete's mouth twisted in horrible uncertainty. "Well… yuh—yes. Yes! I will!"

"All right. I want to ask you one question. Biggers said you were accused of murdering your girl. Did you kill her, Pete? Look straight at me. Did you?"

"No! No, no! I never—"

"You swear that, Pete? Look at me."

"I swear. I swear I never touched—"

"I believe you." Daniels stood still, watching the white wreath of his breath, tense with his own thoughts. "Will you trust me now, Pete? Will you do what I tell you to?"

"What—what you gonna tell me?"

"To give yourself up."

"No! No, no! I won't! They're gonna put me in—in that place—gas—"

"Not if you're innocent."

"They will! They will! They got it all figured! They got my prints right in the room where she was! They know we had a fight that day! They found blood on my clothes! They *will* do it! They'll take me and they'll put me in that place where the gas—"

"They won't if you're innocent. Listen carefully, Pete. I've got about one hundred dollars in my wallet, and here's the keys to this car. If you were lying to me just now, if you really are guilty, I'll give you the money, and you can take the car and make a run for it. That's the best chance you'll ever get—if you're guilty. But if you take the offer, I won't help you any more. I'll be through with you. Take your choice, Pete."

Daniels took out his billfold and extended a flat packet of money and the car keys. Pete's breath rasped in his throat. He grabbed the money and the keys out of Daniels' hand, jumped for the car. He opened the door and stopped short, and stood tensely there, swaying a little. Then he slammed the door shut suddenly and sat down on the runningboard. He put his head in his hands and started to cry with child-ish, shuddering sobs that racked his scrawny body.

Daniels sighed lengthily. The strain had been so breath-taking that he could feel the perspiration moist on his fore-head in spite of the biting cold. He took the money and the keys out of Pete's lax fingers, pocketed them.

"Come on, Pete," he said gently. "We'll go up to Wiles' lodge and call the police. They're probably right on your trail. You couldn't have got up here without leaving traces they could follow. Why in the devil did you come clear up here?"

"I—I used to live—up here. I figured I could hole up in some lodge where nobody was livin'. Lots of people only come up in the summer."

Daniels shook his head slowly. "Pete, the police would think of that the first thing. They'd have dug you out in a day, and I'm willing to bet you wouldn't have gotten ten miles in my car without being picked up. You didn't have a chance."

"I—I didn't never have no chance."

Daniels' voice was hard and flat and determined. "But you're going to get one now. Come along, Pete."

5

DEATH TAKES ONE

THE LODGE WAS a high, dark building, and it seemed to rise out of the white, misty blanket of the snow in reluctant little jerks as Daniels and Pete Carson walked up the twisting slope of the path toward it. There was a long porch on one side, the snow drifted almost level with its railings, and windows along the wall behind it. The drapes were pulled shut and light peeked out in sly, narrow slits.

Pete Carson stopped at the foot of the steps. He stood there small and shivering and scared, his thin shoulders hunched, staring up at the dark bulk of the lodge.

"What's the matter, Pete?" Daniels asked.

"You—you won't...."

"I won't let you down. Come on."

Their feet squeaked coldly on the steps, thumped across the snow laden boards to the front door. Daniels found an iron knocker and hammered it emphatically. The sound rolled away like a drumbeat in the silence.

There was no sound of footsteps inside, but the door swung suddenly back and shot bright light in their faces. The man who had opened it was tall and thin, stooped a little, and he was holding a big revolver in his right hand.

"Who're you?"

"My name is Daniels. James A. Daniels. I think my wife is staying here."

"Daniels!" the tall man exclaimed. "We didn't expect you! But come in! Come in!"

Daniels stepped through the door, and Pete Carson sidled through behind him.

The tall man slid the gun back in his pocket. "I'm Doctor Morris, Mr. Daniels. It's a pleasure to meet you. I've heard a great deal about you "

He had a narrow, long face with aquiline features. His eyes were grayish blue, wide-set and candidly intelligent, and his hair was a shining, burnished white, thick and straight. He had a gray mustache that made a penciled line above lips that were thin and flat and cynically twisted at the corners.

He went on: "Your wife has already retired. We were out skiing all day, and she got pretty fagged out. I imagine she's asleep. Shall I go up and tell her you're here?"

"Wait just one moment," Daniels requested. "I have to make a very urgent telephone call first. Have you a phone here?"

"Surely. In the other room. By the way, I'm sorry I greeted you by waving a gun in your face. There's a murderer loose up this way somewhere, and I didn't feel like taking any chances…."

Daniels nodded. "I know. Here he is."

Morris jumped back, clawing for the revolver. "What! You—he—"

"Don't be a fool," Daniels said coldly. "He happens to be my client. I brought him up here to surrender to the authorities."

Morris' thin face flushed slowly. "I'm very sorry, Mr. Daniels, for my display of nerves. I'm not used to being introduced to murderers in such a casual and unexpected way."

Daniels shrugged. "Pete is not a very desperate character. In the first place, he's not a murderer, and in the second place he's pretty hungry, cold and miserable right now. Is there a place here where he can be a little more comfortable?"

"Certainly. This way."

THEY FOLLOWED HIM through a wide door into an enormously high, long room that ran the whole length of the lodge on the south side. A fireplace filled the whole wall at the far end. There was a log all of ten feet long burning in it now, crawling with bluish, hungry flames. That was the only light in the room, and the shadows wheeled deep and soft and dark in the corners and among the long polished beams against the ceiling.

A man sat stiffly immobile in a chair that faced the fire. His back was turned, and the edge of a heavy white blanket draped over one of his rigid shoulders. He didn't make any move to look toward them.

Morris jerked his head to Daniels, walked over beside the chair. "Blair, this is Mr. Daniels—Cora Sue's husband. He has arrived unexpectedly with a guest who is temporarily a fugitive from justice. Mr. Daniels—this is Blair Wiles."

The man didn't turn his head. He turned his whole body, inching it stiffly around in the chair until he could face Daniels. He was almost completely covered with the blanket, and his body below his shoulders was gross and heavy, limp with a loose lifelessness. His face was a horribly crisscrossed mass of scars—reddened, ugly, deep scars that pocketed the shadows from the fireplace and moved them like groping black fingers across his mutilated features. He wore a black patch over one eye, and the other one was a dilated reddish-white ball set deep in scar tissue. His voice came thick and harsh, straining at the chords in his throat.

"How do you do, Mr. Daniels. It is a surprise to see you here. I understand from your wife that your business affairs were too pressing to allow you to leave. I heard the words 'murderer' and 'client' used in your conversation with Doctor Morris. Were you referring to Pete Carson?"

"Yes."

"He is here with you?"

"Yes."

"Are you in the habit of bringing murderous clients with you when you make social visits?"

"If I choose," Daniels said flatly. "If you wish, we will leave at once."

Wiles' one reddened eye watched him, unblinking. His gross body was unstirring and lax under the blanket. Daniels stared straight back at him, coldly, and the silence grew until it was like a heavy hand laid over the room.

Wiles said: "You are very quick to take offense, Mr. Daniels. And I am regretfully short-tempered due to certain—bodily defects that are no doubt obvious to you. I ask your pardon."

"Surely," Daniels said. "Pete, come up here close to the fire and get warm."

Pete edged up beside them. He stood there shivering in his inadequate overcoat, his hands pushed out timidly toward the flames. He looked pitifully like a stray cur, mangy and down-at-the-heels, cringingly ready for an unexpected blow from any quarter.

"You," said Blair Wiles. "Pete Carson."

Pete swallowed. "Yes, sir, Mr. Wiles."

"Why did you kill that girl, you fool?"

Daniels said shortly: "He didn't. And if you have any questions concerning the matter, address me. I'll answer you, if I see fit."

Wiles lips moved in a grotesque travesty of a smile. "You *are* blunt, aren't you, Mr. Daniels? May I ask how you contacted your client? We had information just a short while ago that he was at large in the vicinity."

"I didn't contact him. He found me. He was looking for me. That's why he ran away from the officer who had him in custody. He wished to persuade me to take his case."

Pete stared, open-mouthed.

Morris chuckled. "You ought to prepare your client for those little surprises, Mr. Daniels."

Daniels turned around slowly and looked at him.

Morris held up one hand quickly. "No offense. That was a poor attempt at humor. We all seem to have got off on the wrong foot here. I'm sorry for my part in it."

"And I for mine," said Wiles. "You are my guest, Mr. Daniels. Please forgive me for being remiss in making you feel welcome. Morris, get some brandy."

Morris went over to a side-table and brought back a tray with a crystal decanter and glasses on it. Daniels poured some in a glass and handed it to Pete. He took another glass for himself. Morris started to turn away with the tray, and Wiles said:

"Give me some."

Morris smiled wryly. "Speaking as your doctor, Blair, you've had enough for tonight."

Wiles voice didn't change in the slightest. "Give me some brandy." Laboriously he brought one stiffened, scarred hand from under the blanket, extended it.

Morris shrugged and put one of the glasses in the hand. He poured some brandy in the glass.

"More," said Wiles.

MORRIS POURED IN some more with a resigned gesture. Wiles raised the glass toward Daniels and then tipped it up to his lips. He didn't bend his neck at all, and some of the brandy spilled out of the glass, ran down his chin. He wiped it off with his scarred hand. Daniels nodded and drank his brandy. Pete sputtered and coughed getting his down.

Morris came back from the side table and said: "By the way, Mr. Daniels, if you will look closely you will see another guest over on the couch in the corner. I neglected to introduce you before because he is not conscious at the moment."

The couch was draped in the shadows that crawled along tie polished walls. The man on it was enormously long and thin. His grotesquely oversize feet extended over one end and hung there laxly, their long toes pointed at each other. He had thin sandy hair and a jutting beak of a nose. One skinny arm trailed down on the floor, and his mouth was wide open.

"Mr. Foley," Morris said. "His wife is around the premises somewhere, too. They are an interesting pair. Every time they go out together they have a race to see who can pass out the quicker. I think Mr. Foley won tonight's contest by about five minutes. He is the source of our information about Pete Carson. Incredible as it may seem, he is an honorary deputy-sheriff, and the authorities called him to tell him to be on the lookout for the fugitive. He lives three or four miles further over toward the lake, and his servants called here to relay the information."

Daniels nodded absently. He had heard a sound outside, and he had turned his head slightly now, listening with an intent expression on his face. He heard the sound again—a faint, distant shout.

"Pete," he said. "Come here."

He walked over to the couch, picked Foley up by his gaunt shoulders and shook him violently. "Wake up! Come on! Wake up!"

"Blub!" said Foley, choking. "Huh? Wha'?"

"Wake up!" Daniels shook him more violently.

Foley's eyes opened. They were wide and blue and glassy and had no more comprehension than the painted eyes of a wax store-dummy. But his voice, surprisingly enough, was clear and quite precise.

"How do you do, sir? Have I met you before and will you allow me to buy you a drink?"

"No!" Daniels said emphatically. "Listen. This is Pete Carson, my client. He is surrendering himself to your custody as an officer of the law here and now. Do you understand what I'm saying?"

"Most certainly," said Foley. "If I may say so, sir, your argument is logically precise, but I must insist that your conclusion will be necessarily false and misleading because your premise is founded on a fallacy. Will you let me buy you a drink?"

"No."

"Thank you," said Foley. "I will have one, too. Waiter, bring another bottle."

Daniels let go of his shoulders. Foley instantly flopped back in the couch and closed his eyes, apparently picking up his stupefied sleep at the exact point it had been interrupted.

Daniels said: "Pete, sit down here beside him and stay there." He turned to look at Morris and Wiles. "You are witnesses that I have formally and voluntarily surrendered my client to a qualified officer of the law."

Morris was grinning. "Mr. Daniels, you are certainly a most resourceful man."

DANIELS DIDN'T PAY any attention to him. He was listening again with taut concentration. Suddenly there was another shout from outside, much closer this time, and then the beat of footsteps on the porch. Something hammered violently on the outside door, and before any of them could move it opened with a resounding crash. A burly thick-shouldered man thrust into the room, holding a rifle ready across his hip.

"Hah!" he said in a triumphant bellow. "Got you, you little rat! Put up those hands!"

Daniels said: "One moment. Just who do you think you are?"

There was a vitriolic bite in his voice, and the burly man stared at him, taken back for a second. He wore a lumberjack coat of crimson and black plaid, corduroy trousers, and high boots. He had a hunting cap pulled down over his ears. His face was as red as the plaid on his jacket, and he had a drooping yellow mustache that partially concealed the thick-lipped looseness of his mouth.

He swung his rifle around. "That—that's Pete Carson! He's a murderer...."

"I'm very well aware of who he is. Who are *you?*"

"Why, Grimes. I'm the sheriff...."

"Can you prove it?" Daniels asked coldly.

Doctor Morris chuckled, wryly amused. "He's the sheriff, all right."

"I'll take your word for it," Daniels said. "Now, Grimes, what do you mean by acting in this manner? Are you aware of the fact that you have just committed two felonies—and very serious ones?"

Grimes' lax mouth opened. "Me? Two—felonies?"

"Yes. For one—assault with a deadly weapon."

"Me? Why, I never touched..."

"You don't have to touch anyone. An assault is an attempt—I said, *attempt*—coupled with the present ability to commit a violent injury on the person of another. If you assault anyone with a deadly weapon, it becomes a felony, and you're pointing that rifle at me right now."

Grimes jerked his rifle aside hastily. "I didn't mean...."

"Besides that, you're guilty of burglary."

"Burglary! I am not! You can't say I stole—"

"You evidently aren't very familiar with your own penal code. I'll quote you its definition of burglary: 'Every person who enters any house, room, apartment, tenement, shop, warehouse, store, mill, barn, stable, outhouse or other building, tent, vessel, railroad car, mine, or any underground portion thereof, with intent to commit grand or petty larceny or *any felony* is guilty of burglary.' You entered here with the intent to assault someone with that rifle, which is a felony, and the proof of that is that you did so assault me."

"It's a lie!" Grimes yelled. "You can't say that! I came in here to get Pete Carson, and I got a right to do it because I seen him through the window, and he's a fugitive—"

"He is not. He's at present in the custody of a properly qualified officer, to whom he surrendered voluntarily."

"Huh?" Grimes said, amazed. "Who?"

"Mr. Foley, there."

"Why, he's asleep!"

"There's no law in this state," Daniels said precisely, "that requires an officer to stay awake after he makes an arrest."

Grimes had recovered himself, and his red face slowly turned a rich purple. "Why, damn you! You can't talk to me that way! I'll show you—"

"Whoa-up!" Morris said quickly. "Don't get in over your head, Sheriff. This man is James A. Daniels. He's Carson's lawyer, and also he's A.J. Bancroft's son-in-law, and A.J. Bancroft has more cash assets than the United States Treasury and a nasty disposition on top of it."

"Uh!" said Grimes, deflating rapidly.

Daniels looked at Morris. "When I want your help, I'll ask for it. I can take care of my clients without aid from you or A.J. Bancroft or anyone else."

"Sorry," said Morris.

Daniels nodded at Grimes. "You can take Pete away now. Be very careful. These gentlemen and myself are witnesses to the way he appears at present. I want to find him looking that well, or better, when I see him tomorrow. If I don't, I'll file charges against you."

Grimes swallowed. "Why—why, I wouldn't lay a hand on him, Mr. Daniels."

"Don't—if you want to go on being sheriff. Now get out. Take him along with you."

"Sure," said Grimes. "Come on, Pete." He took Pete's thin arm and led him toward the door. There he paused and looked back. "—I'm sorry I busted in on you...."

"Quite all right," said Blair Wiles in his thick voice. "Good-night, Sheriff."

GRIMES AND PETE went out, and the outer door made a hollow thud closing after them. Morris gave a little whistle of awed admiration, staring at Daniels.

"You certainly swing a big stick. I'd hate to be on the witness stand with you cross-examining me. Were you really quoting from the penal code—that about burglary?"

Daniels nodded. "Yes. I went to law school in California, and I had occasion to memorize lots of the sections at one time or another. I have never forgotten them. I'm sorry to seem so abrupt with the sheriff, but I believe in impressing officers that my clients are to be treated with care and that I'm not fooling about it, either."

Morris chuckled. "You certainly impressed Grimes."

"And me," said Blair Wiles. "If I ever get into trouble, I shall certainly remember you, Mr. Daniels. I like the way you protect your clients."

Daniels said: "I believe in seeing that they get every protection the law allows them. That is my sworn duty as an attorney...."

"Jim."

It was Cora Sue. She was standing in the doorway that led into the hall. Her blond hair was tousled, and she looked like a sleepily indignant child. She was wearing a blue dressing gown and blue bedroom slippers with white fur on them.

Daniels went toward her quickly. "Cora Sue, honey!" He put his arms around her and held her close. "I came as fast as I could to apologize, dear. I'm sorry for the way I talked to you. You were right. I did need a vacation—badly. Forgive me?"

Cora Sue pushed herself away. "I heard some shouting down here. It woke me up. I heard your voice, too. What were you doing?"

"Well, I…."

"He was protecting a client," Morris said, "and doing a darned good job of it, too."

"A client!" Cora Sue echoed. "Who?"

Daniels swallowed. "Well, Cora Sue, it's a man by the name of Pete Carson. I met him on the way out. He's accused of murder…."

"Murder!"

"Well, yes. He's not guilty, though."

"So," said Cora Sue. "You come out here for a vacation, and the first thing you do is get involved in a murder trial."

"But, Cora Sue, he's just a kid, and he's not getting the breaks. Honey, I couldn't stand seeing him get pushed around like he was just because he didn't have anyone to go to bat for him…."

He had started in a rush of words, but now, looking at her pale, set face, he paused uncertainly.

"Jim," said Cora Sue. "I'm mad. I'm good and mad at you. And I'm tired, too. I'm going back to bed. I'll talk this over with you tomorrow when I feel better."

She turned and marched back through the door, her slim, small shoulders held stubbornly erect. Daniels stood there forlornly and watched her go.

"Never mind," Morris said soothingly. "It happens in the best regulated of families, Mr. Daniels, I can assure you. Would you like another brandy?"

"Yes," Daniels said dully.

He walked across to the fireplace and stood there with the glass held in his hand, staring blankly at the windows. And then he was not staring blankly any more, because there were eyes staring straight back at him.

THEY WERE OUTSIDE, behind the slick shine of the window pane. They were narrow and malignantly steady. They were peering through the small space, like a thin inverted V, where the bottoms of the drapes didn't quite meet each other.

Daniels straightened up incredulously. He could see the rest of the face, besides the eyes, and there was something the matter with it. It was grotesquely swollen and shapeless, and it had no features at all. It was white.

Then Daniels suddenly realized why it looked that way. It was bandaged. It was completely covered with bandage, wound around and around it, until only its eyes were visible.

The glass slipped out of Daniels' stiff fingers and shattered on the hearth. The bandaged face was gone, quicker than the flick of an eyelid, and the windowpane was shining and as blank as if there had never been anything behind it.

Blair Wiles had turned his stiff, unwieldy body to peer at Daniels, and Morris said:

"What's the matter?"

"There was someone—looking in that window...."

Daniels turned and gestured silently. With an effort he got hold of himself now; he was irritated that his voice should have been so hoarse and uncertain an instant before.

"Where?" Morris demanded incredulously. "I don't see—"

From upstairs, Cora Sue screamed. She screamed once and then again, in a rising crescendo of terror.

Daniels spun away from the fireplace, darted for the door. He was in the shadowed length of the hall, and at the back he saw the latticed pattern of a stairway. He went up the stairs four at a time, lunging with reckless haste. At the top there was another and longer hall running at right angles to the lower one.

Cora Sue was standing halfway down it in front of an open door. She was standing rigid, staring into the doorway, one hand pressed flat against her lips and the other out in front of her as though she were trying to push something namelessly horrible away from her.

Daniels caught her shoulders. "Cora Sue! Are you hurt?"

"No! No, no! Mrs. Gregory...."

It was the first time Daniels had known that Mrs. Gordon Gregory was already one of the guests at the lodge, and he turned around now and saw her in the bedroom beyond the doorway. She was lying across the bed, rigidly, on her back.

Daniels let go of Cora Sue and went into the bedroom step by step. Mrs. Gregory was wearing a pair of blue silk pajamas. The top had been ripped cleanly down from the V of the neck and thrown back. Her face was in the shadow, and her slim body looked startlingly like that of a young girl. Her breasts were small and high and firm, and there was a reddened, narrow slit in the white skin just below the left one. Blood had slipped down away from it and coagulated on the flat tautness of her stomach.

From the door, Morris said: "What—what—Oh!" He came in quickly and leaned over Mrs. Gregory. He looked at the wound and then took hold of one of her lax wrists. He let go of it instantly.

"She's dead."

Daniels stood rigid for a second, and then he whirled and jumped for the door. Cora Sue caught at his arm, trying to stop him.

"Jim! Wait! Where—"

"Stay here!" Daniels shouted over his shoulder.

His feet made a rumbling thunder of echoes going down the stairs and the length of the lower hall. He flung the door open, and the wind carried a thin, cold mist of snow in his face. Holding up one arm to shield his face, he went sideways along the porch, staring down at the floorboards, and in a second he found the blurred impress of feet there.

The tracks stopped under the window, turned abruptly away and went to the railing. Snow had been knocked off the top rail, and Daniels leaned over it. There were more tracks below, on the ground, and he vaulted the railing, careful not to land in them.

The tracks plowed away through the drifts, a blurred path that angled and staggered, as though the person who had made it was trying to run desperately fast. Daniels ran, too, fighting the crusted drifts that caught him thigh-high and held him stubbornly back.

He was scarcely conscious of the biting cold as he plunged on through the thick snow. All he felt now was a kind of baffled anger at these drifts which gripped his legs each step and twice nearly threw him on his face. But he stumbled ahead, his eyes on the tracks, like a dog clinging to a scent.

The tracks hit the path where it angled up the rise of the slope in front of the house, and Daniels stopped when he broke through the drifts into it and knelt down trying to see whether the tracks followed it on down the slope, or went back toward the house later.

A cold, smooth voice said: "Put up your hands!"

Daniels drew in his breath with a startled gulp. He raised his hands slowly to the level of his shoulders.

"Now stand up."

The voice was almost polite, but it held a dangerous assurance.

Daniels carefully straightened to a standing position. He half turned, staring back over his shoulder.

"You!" he gasped in incredulous recognition.

6

JIM TAKES STEPS

"INDEED YES," SAID Prince Dak Hassan. "It is I. But who—oh, it is Mr. Daniels. I didn't recognize you. This is a pleasure, I assure you."

Daniels asked: "Could I put my hands down now?"

"Oh, certainly! You must pardon me. You really must forgive me for speaking so abruptly."

Dak Hassan was standing about ten yards down the path, and he looked as neat and dapper and correct as a clothing advertisement in a magazine. He wore a dark homburg tilted rakishly over one eye and a plaid overcoat. The small automatic glinted in his right hand, and he slid it into the pocket of his overcoat now and smiled with a sudden flash of white teeth.

Daniels watched him narrowly and then knelt again in the path and struck a match with numb, cold fingers. The flame flared high for a second, puffed out in the wind, but it had given Daniels enough time to see that the tracks he had been following went down the path, toward where Dak Hassan was standing. The wind and the snow were blurring them, wiping them out rapidly.

"Come here," Daniels said.

Dak Hassan strolled up to him casually. Daniels, still

kneeling, struck another match. He noticed that Dak Hassan was wearing gray spats, and that his tracks were much smaller and lighter than the ones Daniels had been following.

"Have you lost something?" Dak Hassan asked politely.

Daniels stood up. "Not exactly. Did you follow this path all the way up from the garage?"

Dak Hassan nodded.

"Did you pass anyone going the other way?"

Dak Hassan shook his head blandly, "No."

"You're a liar."

"Yes," Dak Hassan admitted. "I am, I often find it necessary in our line of work—don't you?" Hassan's insistence that, simply because Jim had married a wealthy woman, they were confrères was beginning to fill Jim with murderous impulses.

"Never mind that. Who did you see going down this path?"

"No one," Dak Hassan insisted politely. "Really, no one at all. It is a very lonely country."

"You didn't get off that path all the way up here?"

"No."

"Then where did you wade in snow waist-deep? You can see it on your coat."

Dak Hassan looked down. "Oh, that. I stumbled against a bush on my way up here."

"It must have been a peculiar bush. It distributed snow very evenly on your coat to the same height on the front and back and both sides."

"It *was* a peculiar bush," Dak Hassan decided. "I wondered at the time what kind of a one it was."

"Put the boots to him, Jeff!" someone shouted;
and Jim sucked in his breath.

Daniels said: "Listen, you saw someone coming down this path. Someone who was running. You got off the path and hid to avoid meeting him. Whom did you see?"

"But I assure you—no one. Regrettable, but true."

Daniels watched him steadily. "Mrs. Gregory is dead."

Dak Hassan smiled. "Is this an example of that peculiar ghoulish jollity you Americans consider humor?"

"No. It's no joke."

Dak Hassan pursed his lips thoughtfully. "Then I'm very sorry, indeed. I could have made her so happy." He sighed. "But Fate is a very mysterious thing. Perhaps it is all for the best."

"No, it isn't. She was murdered."

"How strange," said Dak Hassan. "She was really quite a nice person. One of the nicest, in fact, that I've ever tried to marry. Who murdered her?"

"I'm wondering that," said Daniels.

Dak Hassan smiled at him. "Your tone is suspicious. I beg you do not waste your time suspecting me. Murder is very crude, and whatever else they are, the Dak Hassans are never crude." He ran a gloved forefinger along his upper lip thoughtfully. "This will necessitate a change in my plans. Much as I regret it, my friend, I will have to revoke my promise to you."

"What promise?" Daniels asked, puzzled.

"The one I gave you on the train—concerning my attentions and intentions toward your wife."

"Oh," said Daniels. "So now you're going to persuade *her* to marry you?"

"Yes."

"Thanks for telling me."

Dak Hassan waved his hand. "Quite all right. I regret it, exceedingly, but this is a cruel, commercial world and one must do one's best with what one has. I will persuade her to settle a substantial sum on you when she divorces you."

'You're very kind," said Daniels.

"Not at all, not at all. It is only fair.

She has so much money—even I won't need it all. Shall we go up to the house?"

DANIELS LOOKED DOWN at the tracks on the path. They were already indistinct, and he knew they would be completely drifted over in a few short minutes. It was useless to try and follow them further.

"Yes," he answered. "By the way, how did you get here so quickly? The train didn't get in until eight o'clock tonight, and it's a day's drive up here."

Dak Hassan moved his shoulders. "Oh, I didn't come in on the train. When it stopped at Reno, I met a girl in a bar across from the station and persuaded her to fly me here in her plane."

Daniels stared at him skeptically. "That train only stops at Reno for eight minutes."

"Eight minutes," said Dak Hassan smoothly, "is quite long enough for me to impress my personality on a woman."

"Oh, I see."

Dak Hassan nodded to himself. "She was a very charming girl, in many ways. She flew me to San Benito. She is waiting there for me. I promised I would come back tomorrow, but of course I won't."

"Of course not," said Daniels.

"After all," said Dak Hassan, "she has barely a million dollars."

"How sad."

"Indeed yes," said Dak Hassan, sighing.

They went up the broad steps to the front porch, and the door swung open with a sudden cold creak of hinges. Doctor Morris peered out at them. "Daniels! You all right?"

"Yes," said Daniels.

"What did you run out for?"

"I was looking for someone I saw through the window. I found his tracks, but I didn't find him. I ran across this instead."

"How do you do?" said Dak Hassan. "Are you Blair Wiles?"

"No," Morris answered blankly. "I'm his physician."

"Oh," said Dak Hassan, losing interest. "Then, may I ask, where is Mr. Wiles? I wish to present myself to him."

Morris pointed. "In there." He said to Daniels: "I've told

Blair about it and called the sheriff's office. They're sending someone up here at once. You didn't catch even a glimpse of that fellow outside?"

"Not when I went out—no. He got clear away."

Cora Sue called from the top of the stairs. "Jim! Jim!" Her voice was frightened and taut with strain. "Are—are you all right?"

"Yes," Daniels answered. "I'm coming right up, dear. Stay there."

Dak Hassan had gone into the living room, and they heard his smoothly polite voice saying: "Mr. Wiles? I am delighted to meet you. I am Prince Dak Hassan. You have heard of me, no doubt?"

Blair Wiles' voice came thickly. "I have—to my regret."

"Thank you," said Dak Hassan. "I would like some brandy." Glassware clinked lightly, and then he said: "Ah, yes. It is quite good. Quite good. Will you have some?"

"I will," said Blair Wiles. "A lot of it."

Morris swore under his breath and said: "I'll have to try and stop that. Excuse me."

HE WENT INTO the living room, and Daniels went down the hall and up the polished stairs. Cora Sue was waiting for him at the top. She had been crying, and the tears had made glistening, crooked streaks down her cheeks. She clung to him wordlessly for a moment, catching her breath in sobbing little gasps, and then she said:

"Where—where did you go?"

"I saw someone outside. I was looking for him. I didn't find him, though."

"Was he—was he the one...."

"I don't know. He—"

Daniels stopped, staring down the hall. He had caught
a slight movement in the shadows at the back, and as he
looked now he could make out a white face peering fear-
fully around the corner.

"Who's there?" he said sharply.

Cora Sue gasped, crowding closer against him. "What—
Oh! It's just Annie, Jim. The cook."

"Come here, Annie," Daniels said.

She appeared around the corner a cautious inch at a
time. She had a fat, doughy face above a ludicrous tent of
a white nightgown. Her stringy gray hair was done up in
metal curlers that glinted in the dim light. Her colorless
eyes were dilated with terror.

"Y—yes, sir. Yes, ma'am."

Daniels said: "Listen, Annie. Mrs. Gregory has been
killed."

Annie's voice rose to a shriek. "Killed! Oh, oh! oh!"

"Stop that!" Daniels ordered impatiently. "Did you hear
anything unusual?"

"I just heard some trampin' and shoutin', and then somebody screamed...."

Daniels nodded. "I know. Did you see anyone?"

"N—no, sir."

"Where are the rest of the servants?"

Cora Sue explained: "There's only one more, Jim. The
chauffeur. He's Annie's husband."

"Where's he?" Daniels asked Annie.

"That bum," said Annie, forgetting her fear. "He's asleep."

"Through all this?" Daniels asked incredulously.

"Once he gets goin', you couldn't wake him up with
less'n an axe."

"Go wake him up," Daniels ordered. "Use an axe, if you have to, but wake him."

"Yes, sir."

Annie padded back the way she had come. Morris came up the stairs. His lips were drawn into a thin, flat line, and there were two spots of color high on his cheekbones.

"Damn him," he said angrily. "Let him drink himself to death, then, and see if I care. I'm getting sick of being insulted. Who's that scum you brought in?"

"Dak Hassan," Daniels told him.

"Dak Hassan!" Cora Sue repeated, startled.

Daniels nodded. "Yes. Calls himself a prince. Do you know him?"

"Surely. He knows all us Dun and Bradstreet girls. Mrs.—Mrs. Gregory told me that she was his latest target...."

"Not any more," Daniels said grimly. "Dak Hassan has made a quick recovery. He told me, after I told him Mrs. Gregory was dead, that he has now decided to marry you. I thought you'd like to know."

"Me?" Cora Sue said, shocked. "And you let him— You didn't...."

"I didn't have time to bother with him," Daniels said shortly. "I've got more important things to think about than Dak Hassan."

"And—and more important—than I am, Jim?"

Daniels made an angry gesture. "Listen, Cora Sue, Dak Hassan considers me a rival. He keeps telling me we're in the same business—marrying money. But I don't consider that to be my career. Would you mind now if I got on with my work?"

Cora Sue swallowed hard. "Oh, Jim! Did he—did he really say that to you?"

"He did. At great length. There was something said about another guest—Mrs. Foley. Where is she?"

"She's asleep, Jim. She—she's drunk."

"Are you sure she's actually drunk?"

Morris said: "Yes. I am, anyway. She drank five martinis before dinner and a fifth of scotch afterward. I was watching her in admiration. Her capacity is amazing."

"All right," Daniels said. "Cora Sue, will you go see if you can't bring her around? The sheriff's men are on their way here. Morris, will you come in here with me?"

Morris followed him into Mrs. Gregory's bedroom. "What do you intend to do?"

"Look around."

Morris looked doubtful. "You're not supposed to disturb anything in a case like this until the police arrive, are you?"

"There's no law to that effect. That's merely a working rule to aid the authorities in investigating. I won't disturb anything that will interfere with them."

"Oh. Daniels, I don't want to seem impertinent, but just what reason have *you* for doing any investigating here?"

DANIELS WAS GETTING a little weary of continual interference, and his voice showed it. "Listen, I have a client whose interests are at stake. He is already accused of one murder, and he was on the grounds and in this house this evening."

"But you said you picked him up on the road...."

"The question involved was asked by a person who had no authority to ask it, and my answer was not given under oath, and I didn't know about this when I gave it."

"Oh," said Morris, understanding.

"How long would you say Mrs. Gregory has been dead?"

Morris shrugged. "Two to three hours."

Daniels stared at him sharply. "Are you sure?"

"I'm not an expert at that peculiar sort of diagnosis, but I think that's pretty close. We had dinner about three hours ago, and I'd say she'd been killed immediately afterward. An autopsy will tell more exactly. She left us after dinner." Morris hesitated. "She came upstairs with your wife."

Daniels' voice was impassive. "I see." He leaned down closer over the body, forcing himself to study it closely. "This—this blood, here. It looks strange to me."

"Also to me," Morris admitted. "I noticed it when I first saw the body. It's diluted."

Daniels jerked upright. "Diluted!"

"Yes." Morris came forward and pointed at a drop of blood like a bright red period against Mrs. Gregory's white skin. "See that? That's normal blood. It's not diluted. But this little pool of blood here is. And I think it's diluted with water."

"With water," Daniels repeated absently. He looked up slowly at the windows across the room. "Snow. Melted snow."

"Why yes! That could be it!"

"Daniels said: "If the murderer's hand was caked with snow, when he struck, some of it would be knocked loose—and melt…" He walked rapidly across to the window, and taking out his handkerchief, used it to pad his fingers while he slid the sash up. The wind blew snow in with a wild-whirling sweep. Daniels shielded his eyes from the bite of it, peered downward at the outside sill of the window.

Morris was looking over his shoulder. "Find anything?"

Daniels brushed at the top layer of drifted snow. His fingers touched something hard underneath, and he picked it up carefully. The slope of a roof went down away from the window. He hunched down and peered along the flat surface of the snow on top of it.

There was a groove, almost drifted full of snow now, that went straight down to the eaves and ended there. Morris was hunched down, too, and he saw the same thing.

"Somebody crawled up the roof!"

Daniels nodded. "And slid down again, I think. Could he get up on the roof from the ground?"

"Yes, the snow is drifted up almost to the eaves. It was that fellow you saw, eh?"

"I think so." Daniels was examining the small object he had found on the sill. It looked like a clod of black, oily dirt, and when he pressed hard with his fingers, it crumbled away in sharp, shiny particles.

"What is it?" Morris asked.

"Sand," Daniels said in a puzzled voice.

"Sand!"

DANIELS LOOKED UP. "Yes. Where is there any sand around here?"

Morris shook his head blankly. "I don't think there is any. Perhaps some gravel sand down on the lake shore, but that's under four or five feet of snow now and frozen harder than cement."

"This isn't," Daniels said. The rest of the sand crumbled away between his fingers. He wiped his hand on the side of his coat, and, using the handkerchief again, slowly closed the window. He stood there, frowning at it.

"What, now?" Morris asked.

Daniels said: "I can't figure out how he did it."

"Did what? Got the window open?"

"No. It was probably unlocked. But the wind has been coming from the same direction all evening, blowing directly against this window. Anyone in this room would know it instantly if the window were opened—even an inch."

"Maybe she was asleep?"

"No. The bed is still made. She was just getting ready for bed. She was hanging up her clothes. See?"

He pointed toward the open closet door. On the floor in front of it, there was a wooden clothes hanger with a skirt dropped in a rumpled pile beside it.

Daniels went on slowly: "She was hanging up her clothes. Something startled her, and she dropped the hanger and the skirt there on the floor."

"She saw the fellow at the window," said Morris.

"Perhaps… But he must have been outside the window at the time. He couldn't open the window and jump through and run clear across the room, circling two chairs and a bed, all in the same split-second. Why didn't she *do* something about it?"

"What?" Morris asked blankly.

"Scream, for one thing. Or this." Daniels went across to the bureau beside the closet door. There was a glittering diamond-set purse on top of it. Using the handkerchief, Daniels picked it up and opened it and showed Morris the big revolver that completely filled its interior. "This was in arm's reach, but she didn't make any attempt to get it."

Morris shrugged, bewildered. "Well, what's the answer?"

"There are two possibilities—both unlikely. One is that she knew the man at the window—recognized him."

"What?" Morris said incredulously. "Why, who would she know that would go crawling around on roofs peeking in windows? You saw this fellow's face. What did he look like?"

"I don't know. His face was bandaged."

Morris' breath caught in his throat with a whistling gasp. "Bandaged!"

"Yes," said Daniels, watching him narrowly. "What about it?"

Morris' lips moved stiffly. "Well—nothing. Only—only it seems a little fantastic, doesn't it? A man with a bandaged face, I mean. Hardly believable...."

"Do you know who it was?"

"No," said Morris. "No, I don't." There was a sheen of perspiration on his forehead.

"Sure of that?"

"Of course I am!"

DANIELS SHRUGGED. "ALL right. Come here, then." He walked back to the bed. "Do you know what these marks here are?" He pointed to the twin abrasions on either side of Mrs. Gregory's waist. They were small, straight marks—a deep and angry red where the skin had been rubbed away.

"No," said Morris shortly.

"Could her clothes have done that?"

"You're married. You know more about women's clothes than I do."

Daniels studied him in silence for a moment and then nodded quickly to himself and went out into the hall. "Cora Sue!" he called.

She came out of the bedroom across from him. Her face was drawn and tired looking.

"I've managed to get Mrs. Foley up, Jim. She—she's still pretty drunk."

Daniels nodded. "Thank you, dear. Would you mind coming into Mrs. Gregory's room for a second?"

Cora Sue's face went paper-white. "In—in—"

"Yes. There's a peculiar mark around her waist. I want you to look at it and tell me if any of her clothes could have made it."

Cora Sue drew a deep breath. "Oh! The money-belt made that mark, Jim."

"Money-belt!"

"Yes. She wears it all the time."

"She's not wearing it now, and I didn't see it anywhere in the room. Why on earth was she wearing a money belt?"

Cora Sue shook her head. "I don't know. I saw it on her once and asked her, but she didn't want to tell me, so I didn't say any more about it."

Daniels hesitated, frowning. "Cora Sue, you didn't send her to see me, I know that. But do you know who did?"

"Yes. She told me. My father."

"Your—father?"

"Yes. She often went to him for advice. He and her first husband—Mr. Gregory—were old friends."

Daniels nodded. "I see. Then your father might know… I'm going to call him long distance."

7

DANIELS TAKES THE CUE

THE LIVING ROOM was full of dark, sleek shadow that moved and swayed with the quiet synchronization of a pendulum, seemingly geared to the smooth and ingratiating overtones of Dak Hassan's glibbest voice. He was sitting in a big chair in front of the fireplace beside Blair Wiles. The brandy decanter was on the floor between them, and at measured intervals, Dak Hassan stooped over and got it and poured drinks into his own and Blair Wiles' glasses.

Blair Wiles had hunched his gross, lifeless body lower under the blanket, until only his scarred, somber face was visible. With the brandy, he had taken on an ugly, unmoving stillness, and his one red-veined eye watched Dak Hassan with an unwinkingly malevolent stare.

Foley still slept on the chesterfield. Daniels was sitting near the door beside the telephone stand, waiting for his call from New York. He was holding the receiver loosely against his ear, listening to the crack and hum of the wires and Dak Hassan's sales talk.

Dak Hassan, it appeared, was the hereditary owner of an immense oil field in the province his family had ruled in the old Russian Empire. The province, along with the oil

field, had been confiscated by the present Russian government and Dak Hassan and his family had been thrown out.
Dak Hassan was now proposing that Blair Wiles put up
the money to sue the Russian Government for the confis-
cation in the Hague World Court.

This would cost. Dak Hassan maintained a mere matter
of two or three million dollars, which Blair Wiles could
easily spare, and would return his money twenty times over.
Dak Hassan stated, modestly, that the oil field was worth
several billion dollars. He paused at appropriate times to
let Blair Wiles comment, but Wiles didn't. He merely sat
there glaring.

The line snapped suddenly in Daniels' ear, and the voice
of the operator said:

"Here is your New York party, sir. Go ahead."

"Hello," said Daniels. "Hello—A.J. Bancroft?"

A.J. Bancroft's voice—as thin and raw-edged and vital
as that wiry little money-king was himself—greeted him
enthusiastically:

"Hell, Jim! Hello, son! Are you all right? Is Cora Sue
all right?"

"Yes. Both of us are fine. But I've got some bad news for
you, A.J. You remember Mrs. Gordon Gregory? She was
murdered here tonight."

"Murdered! Murdered! Hell's flinders, son! Are you
sure?"

"Yes!"

"Blow me down, boys!" said A.J. Bancroft. His voice was
thick and a little shaky. "That hits me kinda hard, son. I—I
liked that woman. Who did it?"

"I don't know—yet. Tell me about her."

"WELL, SHE WAS decent folks. She was, really. She was as dumb as they come and too darned good-hearted, but she never did anyone any harm in her life. She was a sucker for any smooth-talking bird who would flatter her. That's why all those marriages of hers. Every one of those guys were rats. She always came to me before she married 'em and I always told her so, but she never believed me. The newspapers never gave her a break, either. They were always after her."

"How did she meet Gregory?"

"He was in a hospital, and she nursed him. Now there was a mangy old rat if I ever saw one. She treated him like a baby. Everything he wanted, he got. She waited on him day and night for ten years. I told him personally that if he didn't leave her his money when he died I'd chase him through Hell with a red-hot pitch fork, and I meant it, too, and he knew it."

"Cora Sue said you sent her to me. Did you?"

"Yeah. Sure. Why not? I warned her about that money—told her it was damned foolishness to be lugging it across country, and she asked me if I knew an honest lawyer—she knew plenty of the other kind—who could be trusted to go with her, I said, sure. I sent her to you."

"Money?" Daniels said, picking up the word.

"Yeah. The hundred thousand dollars."

Daniels gasped. "The hund—" He remembered that the others in the room could hear him and caught himself. "Tell me more about that."

"I don't know much about it. She came to me and asked me to get her a hundred thousand dollars in bills of various denominations. She didn't want any record of it—didn't want anybody to be able to identify or trace any of the bills. She couldn't get that much in a lump in cash without attracting a lot of notice. I could, and I did. I took her personal note for it."

"Did she say what she wanted it for?"

"No. She wouldn't tell me. I knew she was taking it to California with her. I made her get a money belt to carry it in."

"Both it and the belt are gone."

"*Uh!* I told her it was crazy to carry that much money around! Somebody killed her for that money, son. Somebody knew she had it. Nobody found it out from me. She must have told someone."

"Yes. It was the money, I'm sure. You know those diamond rings she wore? They're still on her fingers. Someone was after the—other—particularly and specifically."

A.J. Bancroft's voice was small and thin and cold. "You find that fellow, son. I want to meet him."

"I'll find him," said Daniels. "Sooner or later. I'll call you again if there's any news. Goodbye."

He hung up and looked around. The other three in the room were still in the same positions. Dak Hassan had given up his oil-field proposition now and was trying to interest Blair Wiles in the lost Russian crown jewels, which Dak Hassan's cousin had buried on the top of a remote mountain peak in the dead of night while fleeing for his life. The jewels, it seemed were worth ten million dollars, and Dak Hassan knew the exact spot in which they were hidden and would go dig them up, if he were properly compensated for his time and labor, and split the proceeds of their sale with Blair Wiles. In answer to a questioning grunt, he estimated that his time and labor would be worth at least a million dollars—cash—in advance.

Foley slept on—peacefully and soddenly.

Daniels frowned to himself, chewing thoughtfully on his lower lip. He got up, finally, and went out into the hall. He was on his way toward the back of it, when he stopped short suddenly and looked up. There was a woman on the stairs.

SHE WAS A very small, very thin woman with a head of frizzy blond hair that reminded Daniels vaguely of a yellow snowball. Her eyes were enormous, glassily blue. Her lipstick had smeared a little on her mouth, changing her expression to a cunning, numbed leer.

"Hello," said Daniels blankly.

She moved her head in a careful nod. "Hello. Is that your brother with you?"

Daniels looked on his right side and then his left and then turned around and looked back. There was no one else in the hall.

"Now there's three of you," said the woman. "My, my, my. Just like rabbits."

Daniels nodded, suddenly understanding. "You're Mrs. Foley."

"Am I?" said the woman. She put her forefinger to her smeared lips and considered the matter. "Why, yes! So I am. I was just wondering what my name was." She came carefully down the rest of the steps, steering herself by the railing, and walked up close to Daniels. "Ssssh! Where's my husband?"

"In the other room."

"Is he still asleep? Is he?"

Daniels nodded again. "Yes."

Mrs. Foley clapped her hands gleefully. "Goody! Now we want some snow! Lots of snow!"

She went unsteadily down the hall to the front door and opened it. The wind almost blew her over backward, but she fought it, got out the door. Daniels followed her curiously. He looked out through the door, shielding his face with his arm, and saw her on hands and knees on the porch. She had spread out her skirt and was carefully piling snow in it. She got up at last, holding up her sagging skirt with the snow heaped in it.

"Watch now," she said to Daniels, coming back inside.

Daniels shut the door and followed her down the hall again and into the living room. Dak Hassan stopped talking to Blair Wiles, and stared incredulously at her as she tiptoed carefully across the room to the chesterfield.

She maneuvered her skirt until it was just over Foley's head and then let go of its edges. The snow cascaded down on Foley's upturned face.

There was a split-second's pause and then Foley screamed horribly. He sat up, waving both gaunt arms.

"Ow, ow! Help! I'm drowning! I'm freezing! Help!"

Mrs. Foley collapsed on the floor, laughing hysterically. The sound penetrated Foley's consciousness. He stopped yelling and wiped the snow out of his eyes and stared owlishly down at his wife.

"You!" he said.

Mrs. Foley pointed her finger at him. "See? I told you it was funny. Isn't it?"

Foley combed the snow out of his thin hair, frowning.

"Do you think that was funny?" he asked, looking sideways at Daniels.

"Oh, very funny," said Daniels. "Very."

Foley nodded at his wife. "You're right. We'll use it. Only I think we ought to have feathers, see? But the guy thinks they're snow, and he gets so cold, thinkin' about it, that he gets pneumonia. How's that?"

Mrs. Foley got up and embraced him enthusiastically. "Ducky, that's just swell. It's beautiful!"

"I think so," said Foley in a satisfied tone. He nodded at Daniels. "Don't you?"

"I don't know," said Daniels. "What are you talking about?"

"The gag," Foley said. "The gag."

"Gag?" Daniels repeated blankly.

"Sure, sure. We're gag men. I mean, I'm a gag-man, and she's a gag-woman. We work together. Ever see Milton Merton, the world's greatest comedian, in the movies? We do all his gags."

"You mean, you think of his jokes?"

Foley winced. "No! His *gags!* A joke is something you say—a gag is something you do. Gags are lots funnier. Like when you sock a guy in the mug with a pie, or hit him with a baseball bat, or give him a cigar that explodes. Those are gags."

"I see," Daniels said. "Did you know that one of the guests here tonight—Mrs. Gordon Gregory—has been murdered?"

Mrs. Foley's mouth opened slowly. "That—that isn't *your* idea of a gag, is it?"

"No. It's true."

"Seems to me I remember hearing something about it," Foley said, scratching his head. "When I was passed out, I mean. I always hear things when I'm passed out. Did they catch the bird that did it yet? The bird with the bandaged puss?"

"Bandaged!" Daniels exclaimed. "Did you see him?"

FOLEY NODDED. "YEAH. Peekin' through the window over there. I'm always seein' things when I'm passed out, but you know I never yet seen a pink elephant. I been lookin' for one. If I ever see one I'm gonna shoot him and frame him."

Daniels ignored that. "Did you recognize the man with the bandaged face?"

"Not exactly," said Foley. "How could I with his puss all covered up? But I've seen those eyes cf his somewhere. They were mighty mean-lookin' glims. I wonder where I saw 'em? They looked mean enough to belong to a producer. Let me tell you, mister, movie producers are the biggest crooks on earth! They'd just as soon murder you as look at you. One of 'em *did* try to murder me once—just because I tried out my exploding cigar gas on him!"

Daniels watched him narrowly. "You didn't talk the way you are now when I woke you up awhile ago."

"How did I talk? Like this? My good man, I have had a most adequate and complete formal education. I have attended various and sundry of the most renowned institutions of higher learning in this and foreign countries."

"Like that," Daniels admitted.

Foley nodded. "I always talk like that when I'm passed out. Think nothing of it. I wish I could think where I ever saw that guy's eyes before. Maybe I'll remember the next time I pass out."

"Don't count on it," Mrs. Foley warned Daniels.

Daniels stared at them, his thin face dark and hard and tight. Little lumps of muscle quivered along the clean line of his jaw. He was tired, physically and mentally, and he had a sudden bitter, nauseated disgust for this house and these people. They weren't normal or decent or real. They were fantasies in a nightmare that Daniels groped through blindly, like a man with leaden weights on his hands and feet.

There was a rumbling thunder of sound as someone hammered on the front door.

"I'll get it," Daniels said shortly.

He went out of the room, down the hall, opened the front door. A squat, snow-plastered figure blundered into the hall, slammed the door shut behind it with a blindly groping paw.

"Uh!" the figure grunted. "Sheriff's office."

Through the melting snow mask, Daniels recognized the deputy sheriff, Biggers, who had been in charge of Pete Carson when Daniels had first seen him on the train. Biggers' stolid, red-veined face, appearing by degrees through the melting snow, was a welcome relief to Daniels. Here, at last, was commonplace normality.

"Hello, there!"

Biggers slapped the snow off his hat.

"Howdy, Mr. Daniels? Sheriff told me you was up here. He's sure pretty mad with you. He says you said you were Pete's attorney."

"I am."

"Fine," said Biggers. "That kid needs a break. He's a good kid. Why, you know, he even apologized to me when he beat it."

"How'd he get away from you?"

"Well, we was ridin' home from the airport in a taxi. It stopped at a signal, and Pete just opened the door and hopped out and started runnin'. Just before he jumped, he says 'I'm sorry, Mr. Biggers.' I run after him, but I ain't a very good runner."

"Why didn't you shoot him?"

Biggers grinned shamefacedly. "That's what the sheriff asked. I told him that I wasn't gonna shoot no kid like Pete when all he was doin' was runnin' away. I figured we'd catch him again, easy. I thought he'd head up this way. Doc Morris phoned in a while back and said somebody'd been killed up here "

"Yes. Mrs. Gordon Gregory."

DANIELS WENT ON and told him what had happened in quick, concise sentences. Biggers tugged at the red woolen scarf around his neck, got it off, shed his overcoat and shook the snow out of it while he listened.

"Uh!" he grunted when Daniels had finished. He stared at the floor for a moment, scratching his head, and then looked up at Daniels. "Grimes—the sheriff—he figures to shove this off on Pete."

"Why?"

Biggers shuffled his feet uneasily. "Well, that brings everything out nice and even. It don't hurt nobody that Grimes don't want to hurt."

"Whom doesn't he want to hurt?"

Biggers lowered his voice to a murmur. "Grimes don't

want to tangle with Blair Wiles nor none of his friends. Blair Wiles throws in plenty for campaign funds in this county."

"I see," Daniels said slowly.

"This is gonna be covered up nice and pretty and smooth. The coroner's jury will bring in the right verdict, and there won't be much investigation of the case, on account that Pete is already in the soup for murderin' his girl."

"I was afraid of that," Daniels said thoughtfully. "Pete didn't kill Mrs. Gordon Gregory."

Biggers nodded. "I know it."

Daniels stared at him. "How do you know?"

"When you passed the control station on the road down aways, do you remember the fella in charge of it?"

"Faintly," Daniels admitted, puzzled. "He was a short, stocky man—young. He was wearing a stocking cap and a sheepskin coat."

"Yeah. That was Dan Sheedy. Awhile back somebody come along and cracked him on the head and give him a fractured skull and left him lyin' in a snow bank. He's gonna be awful lucky if he don't get pneumonia on top of his busted head. He ain't conscious, and he ain't got much of a chance to pull through. I was workin' on that when Grimes called me off and sent me up here. I'd been all along the road to where it hits the Playground Highway down the mountain, and I didn't find anybody who'd seen anything. I got the idea now, though."

"What?"

"It was the murderer that done it. The guy you told me about—with the bandaged face. He'd pulled off his bandages when he was gettin' away, and Sheedy recognized him. It sure couldn't have been Pete. He was up here ahead of you, and he stayed with you until the sheriff got here."

Daniels nodded slowly. "I'm sure Dak Hassan knows who the man with the bandaged face is. I can't figure out how he could know, but I'm sure he does."

"Maybe I could scare it out of him."

Daniels shook his head. "No. Don't let his manner fool you. Dak Hassan is hard and as cold-blooded as a snake. He won't talk if he doesn't want to, and he could probably scare up some sort of diplomatic immunity if you went after him too hard."

"Look," said Biggers. "From what you say, I figure it this way. The Gregory woman was killed for her hundred thousand dollars. That alone—never mindin' the Sheedy angle—leaves Pete out of the picture. He didn't have no way of knowin' about that money."

"It wasn't Pete," Daniels agreed. "This murderer is a different sort of person."

"Yeah," said Biggers. "But I can't do nothin' about it. If I get Blair Wiles sore, he can have my job just as easy as snappin' his fingers. That was what Grimes was hopin' when he sent me up here. He was hopin' I'd tangle with Wiles. But I ain't goin' to. It wouldn't do no good."

"I understand."

"So I'm gonna poke around and ask a few dumb questions. On the side I'll pick up as much evidence as I can find. If I get anything you ain't already found, I'll tell you. It ain't right for Pete to be saddled with this. He's got enough trouble, and he never done this murder. I gotta go in now and ask dumb questions."

HE WENT INTO the living room, and Daniels stood still in

the hall, staring blankly at the wall, trying to get some grip on all the events that had happened, trying to make some pattern out of the chaos the night had brought with it. He was standing there, unmoving, when Cora Sue touched his arm.

"Jim."

Daniels turned his head. "Yes?"

Cora Sue was chewing her lip. "Jim... I was wrong about this. I realize now how terribly wrong and unthinking I was. You're not like these people here. I don't want you ever, ever to be like them."

"They're your kind of people, Cora Sue," Daniels said gently.

"No! No! I don't want them to be! I don't want to be like them, Jim!"

"Are you sure?"

"Yes! Jim... Please let us go away from here—together. I don't want to be here any more. Please, Jim. Let's go away—just the two of us together."

Daniels put his arm around her. "We can't, dear."

"But why not? Blair can fix it for us."

Daniels smiled grimly, thinking about the power money gives those who own it. "Yes. I think he could. But, you see, I have a client now."

"A client! But, Jim, he doesn't mean anything to you!"

"Oh, yes he does," Daniels said softly. "He trusted me. He gave himself up to the authorities because I told him to."

"But they'd have caught him, anyway!"

"Perhaps," Daniels admitted. "But he did trust me. I can't let him down now."

"You can! You must! Jim, he murdered Mrs. Gregory!"

Daniels whirled around and caught her by her slim shoulders. "Why do you say that?" he demanded sharply.

Cora Sue was frightened. "But—but—he must have... He was here on the grounds. He's a murderer..."

"Yes," said Daniels. "Someone else thought of that. When did the telephone call come through from Foley's house warning you that Pete was loose up here?"

"B—before dinner."

"How very convenient that must have been—for the murderer."

Cora Sue's eyes were wide and panic-stricken. "Jim! You don't think—someone here...."

"Yes."

"But the man with the bandaged face!"

"Perhaps he's here, too, And I wonder if he was a man."

Cora Sue shook her head blindly. "No, no! Jim, you can't... And then the other man I heard that detective tell you about. The man on the control station who was hurt...."

"Maybe that has some connection with the murder, maybe it hasn't. I don't know—yet."

Cora Sue took a deep, desperate breath. "Jim, don't you understand? You're a guest here! A *guest!* You can't—you mustn't try to involve them with your nasty little murderer!"

"He is my client. Don't you understand that he put his life in my hands, believing in me, trusting me? Do you think the fact that I'm a guest wipes that out? I can tell you that it doesn't. If I think I can help him, I'll involve everyone that I can with my nasty little murderer."

"No, Jim! Please! Listen to me...."

Blair Wiles' thick, croaking voice called: "Mr. Daniels! Oh, Mr. Daniels!"

Daniels went into the living room. Mr. and Mrs. Foley had turned on the light over the big, carved desk in the corner and were busy arguing with each other across it and scribbling on a piece of paper. Biggers stood in front of the fire-place, looking uncomfortably awkward and out of place. Dak Hassan was sitting in his chair, sipping daintily at his brandy.

Daniels walked around in front of Blair Wiles and looked down into his scarred face. "Yes?"

Blair Wiles said thickly: "I have just informed Mr. Biggers that I am tired of this house and its now unpleasant atmosphere. I am going to my place at Desert Sands. It is in this same county. I am inviting all my guests to accompany me. Would you and Mrs. Daniels wish to come?"

"Desert Sands," Daniels said thoughtfully. "Sand. Why, yes, Mr. Wiles. I would be most delighted to accept your invitation."

Cora Sue was standing in the doorway, her lips twisted palely, staring at him with a horrified foreboding and dread. Daniels smiled at her slowly.

8

THE POLITICO TAKES A PARTNER

THIS WAS SAN BENITO, and it was raining. The rain came down in a long, slow, endless drizzle out of clouds that were unmoving, wet and gray and ominous, huddling down close to the floor of the valley, cutting off all view of the mountains. There was no thunder, no lightning, just the dreary, quiet rain.

Daniels came down the street with his shoulders hunched protectively under the weight of his damp over-coat, his feet splatting in the film of water on the sidewalk. He was watching the numbers above the store doors. He went past the one he wanted, turned, and retraced his steps.

The number was painted on the plaster wall, slantwise, beside a narrow, arched passageway. Daniels ducked into it. It was dark and narrow and heavy with the smell of wetness. His footfalls echoed in a soggy clatter.

At the other end of the passageway there was a man standing, just far enough inside so that the rain couldn't reach him. He was leaning against the wall uncomfortably, his hands in the pockets of ragged gray trousers. He wore a torn leather-jacket and a flannel shirt under it. He had on a musty looking felt hat with the brim dipped down over his eyes.

He looked up as Daniels passed him. He was an old man with sunken, wrinkled cheeks and a stubble of sandy-grayish beard. His eyes were close together, and they had a queer dusty brightness.

Daniels nodded at him, half expecting the old man to try to touch him for two bits. But the old man didn't speak. His eyes were sharp and cruel and wary, staring at Daniels' face, and then he bowed his head again and let the brim of his hat hide his face.

Daniels walked out into a patio paved with stones that glistened red in the rain. There were palm trees at its four corners and a fountain in the middle that burbled disconsolately in competition with the rain. Daniels hesitated uncertainly, got his bearings from a directory board, went up a long flight of stairs to a balcony and round it to a black, bolt-studded door. A neat, glass-enclosed sign beside the door said: *Jonathan Smythe—Attorney at Law—Enter.*

Daniels opened the door and went into a small, square waiting room with two grilled windows in the wall to his right. Directly ahead, through another door, he could see half of a large, flat desk with two big feet resting on it. The feet didn't move.

Daniels walked across the waiting room, looked into the office, and stiffened abruptly. The man who owned the feet was lounged back in a swivel chair that was turned a little sideways. His right elbow was resting on the edge of the desk, and his right hand held a big, old-fashioned .45 Colt six-shooter. The high-pronged hammer was drawn back to full cock, and the long shining barrel of the gun was aimed at Daniels' belt buckle.

"Howdy," said the man holding it.

HE WAS AN enormous young man dressed in a blue suit that was too small for him. He was bald, except for a fringe of reddish, curly hair that circled his head just above his ears. He had blue eyes that were candidly wide and amused, and his face was long and soberly mock-solemn.

Without moving either himself or the six-gun, he looked Daniels over carefully from head to foot. Then he nodded. Pointing the six-gun at the floor, he carefully let the hammer down, turned back the cylinder. Then he dropped the gun in the metal waste basket beside his chair and folded his hands judicially across his chest, creaking further back in his chair.

"Come in, Daniels," he invited.

Daniels stepped into the office cautiously.

"Don't mind the gun," the big man said. "I'm waiting for some unwelcome visitors. Sit down."

Daniels sat down in the chair across the desk from him. "You know who I am?" he asked uncertainly.

"Sure. Saw your pictures in the papers this morning."

"Oh, I see. You are Jonathan Smythe?"

"Right."

Daniels said: "I'm afraid I owe you a great many apologies and a lot of explanation. I stepped into Pete Carson's case without any invitation or permission from you, but the circumstances were such that I couldn't consult with you before taking action."

Jonathan Smythe moved one big hand. "Hell, don't apologize to me—unless you're thinking of stepping out again."

"No," said Daniels.

"Good," said Smythe. He grinned and winked one wide,

blue eye. "Listen, Daniels, you're the biggest and best break that ever came my way."

"Why?" Daniels inquired blankly.

There was a newspaper lying flat on the desk, and Smythe reached out and plopped one huge, blunt finger down on a column at the right side of the page.

"See that? It says that James A. Daniels, brilliant young trial lawyer from the East, is to be associated with Jonathan Smythe, local attorney representing Peter Carson."

"Yes," said Daniels, still puzzled.

"I love it," said Smythe.

"What?"

"The publicity. That's the first time I ever got my name on the front page."

"Oh."

Smythe nodded slowly. "And thanks to you, I'm going to keep it there for a while. You see, Daniels, I'm a lousy lawyer. I'm the world's lousiest lawyer. I'm practically no good at all. But I am a good politician."

"Yes?" Daniels said.

"You bet. Only nobody around here knows it yet. I've run for every office in this county. I've never gotten more than six votes. See, I don't belong to the political machine that runs this county. So they give me the merry ha-ha. But now...."

"Now what?" Daniels asked, watching him narrowly. He couldn't quite make Smythe out.

Smythe said blandly: "Me, I'm gonna coast on your coattails. Every time some newspaper guy takes a picture of you, they're gonna see this pan of mine leering coyly over your shoulder. Every time you do a trick, I'm going to be right there to hand you the stage props and get some of the applause. Yes, sir. It's gonna be you and your shadow, Smythe."

Daniels smiled. "How do you know I'm going to do all these tricks?"

Smythe made a tent out of his big fingers. "Because you can. I followed that case of yours where you got the loony girl out of the asylum and freed of a murder charge. I know how you work, if you have to. And in this case, you have to do it. We ain't got anything else, at all, at all. We haven't got one damned witness but Pete himself, and who'll believe him?"

"Do you?"

"Sure. But I'm crazy."

"Why do you think he's innocent?"

"Because Grimes, the sheriff, and Boken, the district attorney, say he's guilty. Those two guys were never right in their lives. If they say he is—he sure as shootin' isn't."

"That's not evidence."

"Nope. But it's the best I can do. Look." He opened a drawer of the desk and took out a big manila envelope. "Here's the whole case outlined for you. Study it over when you get a chance."

DANIELS TOOK THE envelope. "Thanks." He hesitated, turning the envelope over in his fingers slowly. "Smythe, I can't quite get your angle in this. Just what do you figure you're going to get out of this publicity you think the case is going to get?"

"Elected."

"Elected to what?"

"District attorney, for a starter. I'm a candidate, the only one besides Boken. I'm the stooge. That's the reason for the setup in this case. You see, Pete has no dough. I got the case on a public defender assignment that old Judge Pooley handed me. He's the rat that's going to try the case, by the way. He handed it to me because he knew it was a sour one. Boken was going to make me look like a monkey during the trial. Now we'll see who starts climbing trees and scratching himself."

"Maybe there'll be two of us."

"Oh, no," Smythe said positively. "Boken and Pooley are almost as dumb as I am. Not quite—but almost. You won't have any trouble with them."

"I don't know…" Daniels said doubtfully. He was beginning to regret the reputation for courtroom dramatics that the sensational trial Smythe had spoken of had given him. He had no desire to build his future on such a shaky base. "When is the case set for trial?"

"Tomorrow."

"Tomorrow."

"Yeah. See Pete had been in jail quite awhile before he escaped, and the trial wasn't set forward when he did. I might get a postponement, but it'll be tough. Election is coming, and Boken wants to shine in the public prints about now."

"Can you handle the jury selection?"

"Oh, sure," said Smythe confidently. "I know every damned voter in this county. I've shaken hands with all of them."

"All right. You do that, then. Pete and I both are involved in another murder investigation, as you probably know from the papers, and I have some things to do in that line.

I'm going down to Desert Sands, and I'll call you from there tomorrow night."

Smythe nodded. "Okay. I'll catch you the biggest mess of rumdums you ever saw on that jury. Mind if I hand out some statements to the papers?"

"No. Go ahead."

Smythe reared up to his shambling height and extended his hand. "Brother Daniels, you and I are going to make great big deep tracks all over the map of this county! Just wait!"

9

THE DEFENSE TAKES THE COUNT

THE RAIN WAS a gray haze that hung like misty, shining fog under the palm trees in the corners of the patio as Daniels came down the long stairs from the balcony. He started diagonally across the patio toward the passageway that led to the street, and he was halfway across it when he noticed the two men standing close to the wet wall beside it.

They were tall, dark men in slouch hats and overalls and leather jackets. Their faces were both thin and hard and darkly sullen, almost exactly alike except that one of them had a ridged white scar that ran from the corner of his left eye straight across his cheek to the line of his jaw. This one spoke when Daniels approached them:

"Your name Daniels?"

"Yes," said Daniels, surprised.

"You the lawyer fella?"

Daniels nodded. "Yes."

The other man brought his right hand out of his leather jacket and struck at Daniels without the slightest warning. It was a slashing, downward blow, and Daniels caught the dull gleam of metal on the back of the man's hand and knew he was wearing a pair of brass knuckles.

It came so quickly and unexpectedly that Daniels had time to do nothing more than dodge instinctively. The blow missed his face by a fraction of an inch, came down on top of his right shoulder. It was like being hit with a club. It numbed his whole side, and he staggered with the shock of it.

The scarred man hit him from the other side. The blow caught Daniels high on the side of the head. He spun around, slipped on the wet bricks, and went sprawling on his side. Dazedly, he heard a thin, high screech of triumph.

The little old man he had first seen in the passage was there again now, leaning out to glare at him, his dusty eyes bright and malicious and cruel.

"Get him!" he yelled fiercely. "Give him the boots, boys!"

The two other men were coming for him with set, savage grins on their faces. Daniels rolled frantically over, tried to get up to his feet, but the wet bricks gave him no purchase, and he went down again. The scarred man raised his foot to kick.

The shot was a fat, lingering blast of sound. It came from above and in back of them. Daniels was looking at the little old man at the moment, and he saw the moldy black hat flip off his head as though someone had suddenly hit it with a stick. The little old man clutched at it, missed, then grabbed the top of his head with both hands, as though he were afraid it, too, might flip off. He stood frozen that way, staring up, his face slowly turning a dirty yellowish color.

"Hi, Pappy," said Jonathan Smythe. He was leaning casually over the balcony railing, looking down at them. He held the long six-shooter in his right hand.

The little old man mouthed incoherent noises.

"Pappy," said Jonathan Smythe, "you stand right still. I got a bead on your left ear, and if you were to move I might crack you right between the eyes."

The little old man let go of his head and clutched both ears frantically. "D-don't shoot, Mr. Smythe!"

"Call off your dogs," ordered Jonathan Smythe.

"Lee," the little old man said quickly. "Jeff. Come here."

The two men standing over Daniels backed up, one step at a time, until they stood on either side of the little old man.

"Pick up that hat," said Jonathan Smythe.

THE LITTLE OLD man leaned over stiffly.

His fingers were within an inch of the hat when Jonathan Smythe fired again. The hat jumped a foot and a half in the air. The little old man stood rigid, staring at the hat as though it were a snake about to bite him.

"Pick it up," said Jonathan Smythe.

The little old man's hand was trembling so badly he could hardly hold it.

"Pappy," said Jonathan Smythe. "Take a look at that hat. That's what your head's going to look like if I catch you or these other two bums snooping around here."

"Y-yes, sir, Mr. Smythe."

"Get going."

The three of them went very quickly and cautiously out through the passageway. Daniels got slowly to his feet. His shoulder still felt numb, and he moved it cautiously. It didn't seem to be more than bruised. He looked up at Smythe.

Smythe was casually twirling the big six-shooter on his

extended forefinger. "Sorry," he said. "They didn't hurt you, did they?"

"No," said Daniels. "Who are they?"

"Pappy Hyde and his two sons, Jeff and Lee Hyde. They're three of the county's best first-grade rats. I've been expecting them to call on me, but I didn't think they'd tackle you."

"Why did they?"

Jonathan Smythe stared, surprised. "Oh, don't you know? They're father and brothers of Dolly Hyde, the girl Pete Carson is accused of murdering. They've been talking big about what they're going to do to me. I've been waiting for a chance to show them a few tricks of my own."

Casually, as he spoke, he spun the big revolver into the air above his head, caught it by the trigger-guard as it came down and kept it spinning.

"Trick shooting with a revolver is my hobby. Got a quarter with you? Hold it up, and I'll shoot it out of your fingers."

"No, thanks," said Daniels promptly.

Further along the balcony, a door banged violently open, and a man put his head out. "Smythe!" he shouted angrily. "Will you practice your damned shooting somewhere else? How can I concentrate with that racket going on?"

"Okay," Smythe said amiably. "So long, Daniels. Call me tomorrow night. Don't worry about the Hydes. They won't bother you again. They get shy when they smell powder smoke."

"I hope so," said Daniels. "Thanks for helping me out."

HE WALKED THROUGH the passageway into the street. No one seemed to have noticed the shots. Daniels was still a little shaky and dazed from the suddenness with which the whole thing had happened.

He looked both ways along the street, but the Hydes had disappeared as completely as though they had never been. After a moment, he started along the wet street toward the corner and then he stopped again, staring unbelievingly.

There were two women standing across the street. The one facing him he had never seen before. But the other was Cora Sue. Daniels had left her with the other guests at Blair Wiles' lodge when he had come into San Benito. She had not mentioned any intention of following him. Yet here she was now, and there was something about the slim, rigid line of her back and the set of her shoulders that told Daniels that she was very angry.

She was talking to the other woman reluctantly, and now she turned away with a sudden, impatient gesture. But the other woman caught her arm and whirled her back again. Daniels heard the furious, angry drive of her voice:

"You tell me where he is!"

Cora Sue tried to jerk away, and the woman slapped her in the face. It was a swinging, open-handed blow that splatted sharply above the street sound. Cora Sue staggered, half tripped, sagged against a building wall. She had one hand up to her cheek, and her face was twisted with an expression that was half unbelieving surprise, half incredulous, blazing anger. She struck back at the other woman with her clenched fist. Daniels jumped the gurgling stream of water in the gutter and went for them at a dead run.

10

THE LADIES TAKE TO FISTICUFFS

THE UNKNOWN GIRL was clearly more expert in a rough-and-tumble than Cora Sue. She ducked Cora Sue's wild swing expertly and came in with a rush, her own right fist drawn back to strike.

Daniels got there just in time to grip her wrist and whirl her around off-balance.

"Here!" he said breathlessly. "Stop that!" He looked curiously at the angry girl.

She was young and stormily pretty. She had reddish hair under one of those hats, now tilted crazily over her forehead. Her blue eyes were as bright and hard and glittering as ice. She was slim and tall, and she moved with a quick, trained litheness.

And she was very strong. She twisted her wrist and almost broke Daniels' grip on it. Then she struck at his face with an expert left jab. Daniels blocked that one, caught her other wrist and held her.

"Stop it!" he ordered again, losing his temper fast.

"Mister," said the woman in a deadly calm voice, "this is a private fight. Nobody invited you. You let loose of me, or I'll kick you so hard in the stomach you won't be able to eat for a month."

Daniels said: "I'm sorry, but it isn't a private fight. I happen to be your opponent's husband."

"Ho!" said the girl. "Another one, eh?"

"No," said Daniels. "Not another one. My wife has only one husband. Me."

The girl turned her head to look at Cora Sue. "Is he really your husband?"

"Of course he is," said Cora Sue.

"Do you love him?"

"W-why, yes. Certainly!"

The girl shook her head slowly and pitingly. "Then I'm sorry I socked you. It's certainly hell, isn't it, dearie?"

Cora Sue stared in amazement. "Hell?"

"Yeah. To love one of these gigolo bums."

Cora Sue gasped. "Why—why! Don't you dare call Jim a gigolo bum! I—I'll—"

"Here!" Daniels interrupted, sensing more violence on the way. "Just a moment! We're attracting a crowd. This is hardly the place—" He shuffled around rapidly to get himself between Cora Sue and the girl he was holding.

Cora Sue was breathlessly indignant. "She can't say that about you! I—I'll sock her! I'll show—" She pushed unavailingly at Daniels, trying to get past him.

"Cora Sue!" Daniels snapped. "Stop it! I've already been in one scrap today, and that's enough!"

Cora Sue saw the bruise on his cheek where one of the Hyde brothers had struck him. "Jim! Jim! What was it?"

The other girl was relaxed now, and Daniels let go of her and straightened his tie. "Nothing much. Just some other people who had objections to my taking Pete Carson's' case."

Cora Sue said: "Jim I—I'm sorry."

Daniels shrugged. "Never mind." He looked at Cora Sue's erstwhile opponent. "Now would you mind explaining just what this little set-to is all about?"

"Sure not," said the girl. "My name's Mike Riley."

"Mike?" Daniels questioned.

"Yeah. Short for Michaelena, and don't make any cracks. I'm from Nevada, and I'm looking for a guy by the name of Prince Dak Hassan."

"Oh," said Daniels, suddenly understanding. "You're the girl he met in Reno. The one who flew him here."

MIKE RILEY NODDED her head. "Right. He premised to come right back and meet me here at the hotel, and he ditched me. Now I'm looking for him, and I'm going to find him."

"What happens then?" Daniels asked curiously.

"I'm going to marry him."

"Oh," said Daniels. "Does he know that?"

"You bet he does. That's why he's hiding out."

Daniels frowned thoughtfully. "I see. It's none of my business, but do you—know much about this Prince Dak Hassan? Do you know the sort of person he is?"

"You bet."

"And you—still want to marry him?"

Mike Riley set her jaw firmly. "I do."

"But you mustn't!" Cora Sue exclaimed, horrified. "Really, you mustn't do that, Miss Riley! You don't understand. Dak Hassan is a notorious—"

Mike Riley shook a slim, tanned finger at her. "Now, now! Remember how mad you got when I made cracks

Jim had never seen his wife mixed up in a street fight before.

about your husband. It so happens I love the slimy little monkey."

"Oh," said Cora Sue.

"That's why I got mad," said Mike Riley, "when I saw you. I recognized you from your pictures in the papers, and I was sure that little rat had found out you were around here and attached himself to you. I—was trying to scare you off. I really wouldn't have hurt you." She grinned suddenly.

"It so happens," said Daniels, "that the fact you mention doesn't seem to bother Dak Hassan much. He *has* attached himself to Cora Sue."

Mike Riley narrowed her blue eyes at Cora Sue. "Do you love him?"

"For pity's sake, no!" said Cora Sue emphatically.

Mike Riley nodded. "All right. You just tell me where I can find him."

Daniels shrugged. "The last I saw of him, he was still up at Blair Wiles' mountain lodge above Phantom Lake. He was there when I left this morning."

"He was there when I left a little later," Cora Sue put in. "They were all getting ready to go down to Desert Sands, though. I don't know where he is now."

"I'll find him," said Mike Riley firmly. "One place or another—I'll find him."

"Good luck," said Daniels.

Mike Riley nodded her head at Cora Sue. "I'm sorry I socked you. You're pretty nice. And I'm sorry I called your husband a gigolo bum. He isn't."

"Thanks," said Daniels, smiling.

"So long," said Mike Riley gravely. "You'll be seeing me."

She turned away and walked down the street, erect and straight and quick, her head held confidently high.

Daniels chuckled, watching her. "I think Dak Hassan will have his aristocratic hands full with that one."

Cora Sue's voice was anguished. "Jim, why does everybody—*everybody*—have to say nasty things about you and my money? Can't they understand that it doesn't make any difference just because I have money? Can't they understand that I can love you just as much whether I have money or not, and—and that you can love me just as much?"

"People, my dear." Daniels shrugged.

Cora Sue took hold of his arm and held it tightly. "I—I can understand now how you feel sometimes. Everyone throwing that up to you—all the time, all the time! I don't blame you a bit for feeling that way, either! But why can't they let us alone?"

"They never will, Cora Sue," Daniels said slowly. "Never. They'll always be saying those things and whispering them and hinting them. If I ever make a success in my profession, they'll be saying that it was because your money was behind me."

Cora Sue was frightened. "Jim!"

Daniels' smile was bitter and twisted. "I might as well get used to the idea, I guess. Why did you come down here to San Benito today?"

"I was wrong about your taking Pete Carson's case. I wanted to tell you about that. And Jim, I wanted to stay with you. Can't we stay here in San Benito—together? I don't want to go down to Desert Sands—with those others. Can't we stay here—please?"

Daniels shook his head. "No. I'm sorry, dear. I have to investigate the death of Mrs. Gregory. I didn't take her case when she came to see me because I thought you had sent her. She wanted me to come to Phantom Lake with her. Your father sent her to me. She was a friend of his. If I'd come with her as she wanted, maybe she'd be alive now. I promised him I'd find out who killed her."

Cora Sue shook her head blindly. "But—but she was killed at Phantom Lake, not at Desert Sands!"

"I think the answer is at Desert Sands. There was sand in the snow on the window sill of her room." Daniels shrugged his shoulders uneasily. "We can't stand here in this rain. Shall we go have a drink in some warm, dry place? I think I could use one."

Core Sue nodded automatically. "So could I." Her face was white. She watched Daniels with worried eyes.

11

A GAG-MAN TAKES A DRINK

THE COCKTAIL LOUNGE of the Hotel Gregario was supposed to be a reminder of the days of '49, but no old-timer would have recognized it. The bar was slick and black and high, and the tables and chairs had chromium legs. Murals on the walls depicted miners dressed as no miner had ever dressed, panning gold in a manner that would have made a real miner's hair stand on end.

In one corner there was an old-fashioned piano— painted a modernistic egg-shell white now—and Foley was sitting on the bench in front of it. When Daniels and Cora Sue came in he was playing the *Prelude in C Minor* in swing time and playing it surprisingly well. He looked over his shoulder at them and said: "Good morning to you, my dear people," in a gravely cultured tone.

A waiter appeared and ushered Daniels and Cora Sue to a table at the opposite side of the room. Foley retrieved a bottle of whisky from under the piano bench and headed for their table.

"Does he know you," said the waiter, "or shall I give him the old boff?"

"He knows us, I'm sorry to say," Daniels answered.

He and Cora Sue ordered drinks, and Foley sat down

very carefully and slowly in the third chair at their table. His long, thin face was gravely expressionless, and his protruding blue eyes were as round and glassy and unseeing as marbles. He spoke in very cultured and precise tones.

"My two dear young people, I am inexpressibly shocked to discover you in such depraved and wicked surroundings. Let me most solemnly warn you against the evils of drink and dissipation and association with low and uncouth characters before it is too late."

"Thanks," said Daniels. "We'll consider ourselves warned. Wouldn't you like to go and play some more?"

Foley shook his head slowly. "No. You two are my duty. I cannot tear myself away."

The waiter came with the drinks Cora Sue and Daniels had ordered. He said bluntly to Foley:

"Why don't you go home?"

"Home?" Foley repeated oratorically. "Home? The word has no meaning to one who carries the unextinguishable torch of genius within his mighty brain."

"Fooey," said the waiter. "The torch of genius ain't the only load you're carryin' right now."

"Away, away!" said Foley. "Go, varlet!"

"Shall I give him the boff now?" the waiter asked Daniels.

Daniels shook his head wearily. "No. We know him."

The waiter looked at them pityingly and retreated.

Foley stared at them solemnly. "Perhaps you two would like me to give you my short illustrated lecture on the preservation of the tropical fish?"

"No," said Daniels.

"It's a wonderful piece of word imagery. It has been

acclaimed by all the crowned heads of Europe. They ate it up."

"No," said Daniels.

Foley made a notion of washing his hands. "I've done my duty. Have a drink, Foley." He proceeded to tip up the whisky bottle and follow his own advice—twice. He put the bottle down and nodded at Daniels. "Let's get stinking."

"Let's not," said Daniels.

"All right," Foley agreed, taking another drink. "We won't. By the way, I saw our friend this morning."

"Who?" Daniels asked, uninterested.

"The gentleman who gallops about with his face covered with bandages."

DANIELS TENSED. "WHAT? The man with the bandaged face? The man at the lodge last night?" His lean strong hands curled around Cora Sue's fingers.

Foley nodded. "Yes."

"Was his face still bandaged?"

"No."

"Did you recognise him?"

"Oh, yes."

Daniels stared skeptically. "How?"

"By his eyes. They are quite unmistakable. I seem to remember telling you I had seen them somewhere before."

Daniels kept his voice level with an effort. "What's his name?"

Foley shook his head. "I don't know."

"Where did you see him?"

"I don't know," said Foley.

Daniels' lips tightened dangerously. "You're not funny."

"No," Foley assured him seriously. "I really saw him—this morning. And I recognized him at once. But now I can't remember where I saw him or what his name was." He paused to beam at Daniels. "Odd, isn't it?"

"You fool," said Daniels. "Do you realize that the man with the bandaged face is vitally concerned with the murder of Mrs. Gregory? Don't you see how important it is to identify him?"

"Certainly," said Foley. "We can't very well arrest him if we don't know who he is, can we?"

Daniels held himself in. "Foley! Try and remember. Try hard, man. *Who was that man?*"

Foley said: "I think I'll go to sleep now." He closed his eyes and relaxed limply. He promptly fell off his chair and on to the floor. He began to snore.

The waiter came running. "I thought that was gonna happen. When he starts givin' people illustrated lectures, it ain't very far off."

Daniels got up, his face white. "See if you can't sober him up."

"Nope," said the waiter. "Not him."

"How long has he been here?"

"Since we opened up. He was waitin' outside."

"Was there anyone else in here while he was here?"

"Nope. Not until you come."

Daniels turned to Cora Sue, his shoulders sagging hopelessly. "There it is. Right there. The key to this thing. He knows it. If he could only tell us!"

"Maybe when he's sober again…" Cora Sue suggested.

"I wouldn't count on that, lady," advised the waiter. "I got him figured. He's one of these here split personalities. He's one guy when he's drunk and another guy when he's sober. They ain't the same guy. In fact, they ain't even related. When he's sober he never remembers anything he did or said when he was drunk, and vice versa."

Daniels took Cora Sue's arm. "Let's get out of here. When I think of Mrs. Gregory lying murdered, and that fool with the answer... Come on!"

12

THE DEFENSE TAKES A TUMBLE

THE DESERT NIGHT comes with a quick, queer softness, drawing a curtain on the brightness of the day. It was coming now, a blue shadow, limitless and formless, that crept out of the valleys and slid quietly up the red-brown jumble of the mountains.

Cora Sue was sitting in the front seat of the hired sedan beside Daniels. "It—it's wonderful, isn't it, Jim?" she said, staring out across the rolling waste that was covered with a frosting of tough, stunted brush. "It's so desolate and so grand and—and ageless. It makes a lump come in your throat, just looking at it and thinking about it."

The sun made a brilliant farewell gesture on the mountaintops, and the blue shadows thickened and spread over everything, as though an immense brush had painted them in one long sweep.

"Yes," said Daniels absently. He snapped on the lights. The asphalt road was black and slick ahead of them. "We must be almost to Desert Sands now."

A car made a moaning, mournful whip of sound going past them fast in the opposite direction, and after the glare of its headlights was gone they could see a faint glow low against the horizon ahead.

"The wind is warm," said Cora Sue wonderingly. She had the window on her side open, and she put her face close to it, savoring the feel of the air. "And just yesterday—less than a hundred miles away at Phantom Lake—we were skiing in snow that was three or four feet deep. And all in the same county!"

"Yes," said Daniels.

He was thinking of that county and of all the things that had been done there and the things that he had to do as a result. He had set himself an impossible task. He realized that with a feeling of grim bitterness.

He had to fight for Pete Carson's life. That alone would require every bit of intelligence and ingenuity and energy that he had. Then there was the additional inexplicable jumble of Mrs. Gregory's murder. And all the weird nightmare characters that were mixed in it. Blair Wiles, and Doctor Morris and Dak Hassan and Foley, the fool who knew the answer but couldn't tell it.

It was a mess so exasperating, so viciously twisted and obscure that it made Jim sore just to think about it.

The glow on the horizon had become bright now, and as the road turned they went by a service station that was like a brilliant lighted island in the sea of the night. And then there were other islands, coming at closer and closer intervals. Signs that popped up commandingly and were gone.

And then the road swung again and went under a lighted arch with neon letters scrawled emphatically across it:

WELCOME TO DESERT SANDS—THE WINTER
RESORT OF THE WORLD

The main street was long and narrow and straight ahead of them, and every store along it was lit with neon signs that jumped and leaped with fiendish irregularity.

The street was lined with cars, and the sidewalks were full of people all dressed with a colorful uniformity. The men wore polo shirts and slacks. Daniels couldn't see one of them with a coat on. The women all wore either slacks or shorts with blouses or bandanna halters. Everyone had a uniformly dark coat of tan.

"Why!" Cora Sue exclaimed, amazed and delighted. "It's just like the boardwalk, isn't it? Only this is more— more permanent. And look at that shop! And that one! They're branches of the most exclusive stores in the country!" Her eyes brightened as a woman's will when she plans a debauch of shopping. Murder had slipped her mind.

THEY WENT ON, driving more slowly now. They passed a restaurant where people were eating out on the roofless terrace. At the end of the next block the stores stopped as suddenly as they had begun. There were residences here, low and white and comfortable looking. They became further apart, and then the paving stopped. The road curved sharply, split into two separate routes.

"To the right," Cora Sue directed. "Up that canyon."

The road was narrow and bumpy, and the springs on the sedan creaked complainingly. They jounced over a wooden bridge that spanned a dusty ditch.

"Slowly now," said Cora Sue. "We're close to it, I think. There's a sign."

The canyon walls were pinching together, high and austere and threatening on either side of the road. Dusty, grotesquely twisted trees made queer patterns in the glare of the headlights.

"There!" said Cora Sue.

Daniels saw the sign, exactly the size and shape of the one that had guided him to Wiles' place at Phantom Lake. The headlights showed the beginnings of a graveled path beside it. Daniels swung the sedan in and parked it against the bank at the side of the road. When he got out, he could see scattered lights outlining the shadowy loom of a building halfway up the canyon wall.

"That must be it," he said. He opened the door for Cora Sue, helped her out.

They went up the steep slope of the path in the darkness, their feet crunching a little on the gravel. At the first turn, Cora Sue pulled back on Daniels' arm.

"Wait," she gasped. "Wait until I get my breath. I'm no mountain goat, my sweet. Not in these heels."

Daniels stopped, looking up at the steely pin-points of the stars, breathing deeply. It was a queerly majestic sort of country, he thought. Endless and old beyond the conception of man. Terrible in its wide emptiness, and yet fascinating, too.

Cora Sue's clutched his arm wildly. "Jim! There—there's someone on the path—ahead...."

Daniels jerked his head around. He saw it too. Not more than ten feet away. A figure, vague and formless, darker than the night around it. Not moving at all. Standing there with a deadly stillness.

Daniels put his arm out slowly and moved Cora Sue behind him. He could feel her crowded close against him, hear the quick sound of her breathing.

The figure on the path didn't move.

"Hello," said Daniels.

The figure stood there, silent. It was menacing without making any move to be. Its very quietness was dangerous.

"Hello," said Daniels. "Who are you?"

The figure took a step backward, up the path, and the gravel crunched slightly under its foot. It made no other sound. There was no other sound in the whole world.

Daniels drew in his breath. He walked straight up the path toward the figure.

Cora Sue said: "Jim!"

The vague figure crouched, half-turned. It hesitated there while Daniels took three steps, and then he was close enough to see the white splotch that was its head.

It was like an electric shock going through him, and he jerked out the words in a half-shout: "The man with the bandaged face!"

THE DARK FIGURE whirled and jumped sideways off the path. Daniels leaped blindly after it. Brush crackled under his feet, clawed prying fingers across his face. The ground slid away sharply. Daniels went down with half-running, awkward strides, and then a stone turned under his foot. He fell down the slope in a lunging, rolling sprawl.

One of his wildly threshing legs kicked against another leg, and he doubled up instinctively, groping out blinding in the darkness. His hand touched the smoothness of a silk shirt, and then a heavy body landed on top of him and smashed him hard against the ground.

Daniels kicked desperately, and the slope helped him. He rolled over on top of the man with the bandaged face and struck once and then again at the blur of the bandages, feeling the soft give of them under his fists.

The man with the bandaged face swore. He swore in a vicious ugly undertone, and he heaved up under Daniels and threw him off. Daniels stumbled and got to his knees. The man with the bandaged face was kneeling, too, facing him.

"Jim!" Cora Sue called from the path. "Jim!"

Daniels gathered his legs under him, lowering his shoulders for a sudden lunge, but he didn't make it. The man with the bandaged face had a gun in his hand. Its barrel made a cold glitter in the dark.

"Jim!" Cora Sue screamed.

"Damn her," said the man with the bandaged face.

A door slammed in the house above them, and a voice shouted: "What? Who is it?"

The man with the bandaged face turned his head at the shout, and Daniels slapped at his gun hand, hit it and knocked it down. The gun made a smash of sound that thundered away in the night. Daniels dove in low. His shoulder hit the man's ribs.

They went backward down the slope, over and then over again, crashing through the brush. Daniels had hold of the other's arm with both his hands, and he could feel the thick corded muscle in the wrist writhing, twisting, trying to turn the gun around and against him.

The man with the bandaged face found purchase for his feet in the loose, shifting sand. He heaved up, bringing Daniels up with him. Daniels tripped him, and they went down into another sliding, rolling sprawl.

There were other voices shouting from the direction of

the house, coming closer now, and Cora Sue was somewhere above, calling Jim's name again and again.

The man with the bandaged face made a choking,
desperate sound in his throat. He struck at Daniels with
his left fist.

Daniels ducked one blow and another, but the third hit
him squarely between the eyes with sledge-hammer force.
The shock of it loosened his grip for a split second, and
that was enough.

The gun swung round in a swishing arc and came down
on Daniels' shoulder. It was the same shoulder that had
been struck with the blackjack that morning, and this blow
sent fiery waves of pain all down his side. He stumbled, and
his knees gave out under him.

He fell, twisting himself around. His right arm wouldn't
obey. He came down hard on his right side, and his head
landed on a stone half-buried in the ground.

The whole world seemed to rise up and throw him into
pain-sick blackness, but he didn't lose consciousness. His
mind was small and cold and far away, fighting the blackness that numbed him. He got up and fell and got up again,
staggering blindly.

13

THE DOCTOR TAKES THE RAP

THEN CORA SUE came sliding down the slope through the brush and caught him and supported him with her slim, vibrant strength. "Jim! What is it? Are you hurt?"

Daniels shook his head. "No," he said thickly. "Where is he? Which way did he go?"

Sound came from somewhere below them in the darkness. The starter of an automobile groaned on a rising scale, and then the noise of the engine came with a sudden chattering rip. Gears grated, and they heard the spatter of gravel under fenders.

"There!" Daniels exclaimed. "Getting away—car...."

He started down the slope, still staggering, but Cora Sue held on with both hands, dragging him back, digging her high heels in the sand frantically.

"No! Jim, you can't! No!"

The engine sound faded in the distance. Dak Hassan landed beside Cora Sue and Daniels, coming down the slope in quick, effortlessly agile leaps. He was holding his .25 automatic poised in his right hand. He was not even breathing hard.

"What is it?" he asked calmly. "Is there some trouble?"

"The man with the bandaged face," Daniels said dully. "He got away from me."

"How sad," said Dak Hassan. "But you, my dear lady! Look! Your beautiful face is scratched with the brush! You are distressed! It is horrible! Let me help you!"

"Oh, leave me alone!" Cora Sue snapped, batting away his proffered hand. "Help me with Jim. He's hurt!"

"Your sympathy is touching," said Dak Hassan. "So touching, my dear beautiful lady, that it grieves me to see it expended on a mere clod. However, I obey your every wish...."

He took Daniels by his other arm, and between them they helped him up the slope and on to the path again. Pain in wavy, fiery streaks had cut through the numbness that held Daniels' body now, and he was able to think clearly.

"Get to the house," he said. "At once. Got to tell the sheriff—have him cut off the roads."

He went on up the path at a stumbling half-run with Cora Sue still holding stubbornly on his arm.

The house was long and low and white, with a high white wall set flush with the front and circling the grounds behind. There was no porch, only a wide front step with a heavy, bolt-studded door back of it.

The door was open, and Doctor Morris was standing there, tall and straight, his hand shading his eyes.

"What happened?" he demanded. "I heard a shot."

"The man with the bandaged face again," Daniels said.

He pushed past Morris, through a narrow entry hall and into a low, shadowy, comfortable-looking living room. Blair Wiles was sitting in his big chair, wound around and around with blankets, against the far wall that was composed entirely of windows that stretched from floor to ceiling. There was a lamp over him, and its downcast light made a lumpily grotesque mask out of his scarred face.

"Where's the telephone?"

Wiles pointed with a stiff, scarred hand. "There. You seem to make a habit of bringing excitement with you, Mr. Daniels."

Daniels picked up the telephone, jiggled the receiver. Cora Sue and Morris and Dak Hassan made a curiously staring group in the doorway, watching him.

"Hello!" Daniels said into the telephone. "Hello, hello! Operator!"

There was a sudden, sharp scream.

THE OPERATOR WAS talking in Daniels' ear, but he ignored her. He dropped the telephone on its stand with a sudden clatter and whirled around.

"What was that?"

The faces of the others were like white, waxily startled masks staring back at him.

Morris said stiffly: "Sounded—in the back…" He gestured toward a door at the left of the room.

Daniels ran for it, jerked it open. He was looking across another and smaller living room and into a lighted hall beyond. He ran toward the hall, hearing the footsteps of the others close behind him. He spun around the edge of the door and stopped with a jerk.

Annie, the maid he had seen at Phantom Lake lodge the night before, was standing stiffly in another lighter doorway. She was holding a neatly ironed pile of linen in her arms. She screamed again now, and the linen slipped out of her arms and landed in a crumpled, fluttering pile on the floor.

"Annie!" Daniels said sharply. "What's the matter?"

Annie turned a twisted, terrorized face. "In—in there… On the bed."

Daniels pushed her aside, looked in through the doorway. He blew out his breath in a long, whistling gasp.

"This is my bedroom," said Morris, coming up behind him. "What—"

"Look," said Daniels, pointing.

The bed was on the far side of the room under the wide row of windows. There was a reading lamp on a white stand beside it. The lamp was lighted now.

The bed had a tan brocaded spread, and there were two objects lying in the middle of it. One was a belt—a wide, peculiar looking belt curled in a loose circle. The belt had pockets in it. The snaps that covered them were loose, and the pockets were obviously empty. The second object was a short, broad-bladed hunting knife.

"What—" said Morris breathlessly. "What—"

The blade of the knife was stained with something that was black-red, congealed horribly. Some of it had rubbed off on the spread.

"That," said Morris stupidly. "That—is my hunting knife."

Cora Sue's voice sounded small and thin. "That belt—was the one Mrs. Gordon always wore."

"I seen it!" Annie cried out hysterically. "I come in to give him some new towels, and I seen that knife on the bed—all bloody-like! He done it! He's the one!"

"Well, Morris?" Daniels said quietly.

Morris' thin, tanned face was queerly drawn, and a muscle kept twitching in his cheek. "Surely, you don't—don't think—"

"He done it!" Annie screeched. "He's the murderer!"

Morris whirled on her. "Shut up, you—you—"

"So very, very interesting," said Dak Hassan in a thoughtful way.

MORRIS SEEMED TO congeal. He crouched a little, turning around very slowly. Blood began to creep darkly up into his white cheeks, and his voice came in a hissing whisper.

"You. You filthy little rat. You put them there."

Dak Hassan was still holding his small automatic. He backed up a step, raising it. His eyes were warily alert.

"You are a fool, my good doctor. If you were not, you would know I could not have put them there. I did not have an opportunity. I was in the living room with you and Mr. Wiles all evening—until I ran out the front door when I heard this peasant scream."

"He didn't put them there," Daniels said. "The man with the bandaged face did that. That's why he came here. That's why he didn't shoot me when he had the chance. All he wanted was to get away—after he had left these things. Why did he put them on your bed, Morris?"

Morris stared at him. "Wh—what?"

"He had a reason for doing it. What was his reason?"

Morris shook his head, bewildered. "I—don't know. I—I don't know—what you're talking about."

"You're lying," said Daniels calmly. "You know who the man with the bandaged face is. And I want to know, you see."

"I *don't* know!" Morris denied angrily.

"You do," said Daniels. He nodded at Dak Hassan. "And so do you."

"I?" said Dak Hassan, smiling. "But, no! You could not prove that, my friend, No, you really could not."

Daniels watched him narrowly. "I saw a friend of yours today."

"A friend?" Dak Hissan repeated, surprised. "Who?"

"Mike Riley."

Dak Hassan's breath whistled between his teeth. "That one! Was she—was she…."

"Looking for you?" Daniels finished. "Yes, she was. She's going to marry you."

Dak Hassan's smile jerked at the corners. "Marry me! *Me?* But that is impossible! She has no background, no culture, no breeding—*and* no money, or at least not nearly enough. And besides, she does not know where I am."

"Oh, yes she does."

Dak Hassan's voice was a thin whisper "You—told her?"

"Yes."

"You will be sorry for that, I think."

"Not nearly as sorry as you'll be when she finds you. Of course, I might help you out with her. Who is the man with the bandaged face?"

"I tell you, I do not know who he is!"

"You do," said Daniels." And so does Morris. You think you can keep me from finding out, but I'm telling you now that you can't. Do you understand that? You can't. I'll—find—out!" He whirled away from them and started up the hall.

"Jim," Cora Sue said anxiously. "Where are you going?"

"To telephone the sheriff."

14

DAK HASSAN TAKES NOTICE

BIGGERS HAD COME from the sheriff's office in answer to Daniels' telephone call, and he and Daniels were alone now in Morris' bedroom. Biggers was standing beside the bed, staring down at the money-belt and the knife with a sort of gloomy bewilderment while Daniels told him of the things that had happened before his arrival.

"We sent out a call after you phoned," he told Daniels. "Told the boys to be on the lookout for a suspicious car. It wasn't much use, though, since you didn't know what kind of a car the guy was drivin' or what he looks like without those bandages on his puss. This is a hell of a case. It don't make good sense.

"What would that bird want to throw these things on Morris' bed for? Hell's bells, you'd think if he killed that dame, he'd want to bury this stuff somewhere instead of throwin' it around where people would find it."

"That's it," said Daniels. "If."

"Huh?" said Biggers.

"*If* he killed her. I don't think he did. I've had a hunch about that from the first. I can't figure out just where he comes in, but I don't think he killed Mrs. Gordon."

"Why not?" Biggers asked.

"For several reasons. In the first place, I don't think he got up to the lodge until after I did. Mrs. Gordon was killed a couple of hours before that. You remember the setup in her bedroom?

"I said at the time that there were two explanations as to why she didn't cry out or attempt to reach for that gun she kept with her when the man with the bandaged face opened her window. One explanation was that she knew who he was—that she was expecting him. The other explanation is that she *couldn't* cry out or fight. Because she was dead at the time."

"But why did he come inside, then?" Biggers protested. "He could easy see her lyin' there from the window."

Daniels nodded. "He did. And he saw this." He pointed to the knife on the bed. "He recognized it. He knew it belonged to Morris. He came in and got it. When he jerked it out, some snow fell from his hand or sleeve and diluted the blood."

Biggers eyed the knife distastefully. "What would he want it for?"

"I don't know. I'm sure, though, that Morris knows who the man with the bandaged face is. I don't think Dak Hassan does—that is, knows his identity—but I think Dak Hassan knows Morris does."

Biggers blinked. "Come again."

"Morris knows who the man with the bandaged face is. He won't admit it. He has some reason for concealing it. Dak Hassan knows that. He has been trying to blackmail Morris, I think. I guessed that from what Morris said to him when we discovered the knife and the belt here."

Biggers scratched his chin. "Maybe I better talk to them two babies."

"It won't do you any good. Morris won't say anything. Dak Hassan is too slick to be bluffed into admitting attempted blackmail."

"Uh," said Biggers, agreeing. "I wonder how Dak Hassan figured this out if we can't."

"He saw more than we did. He saw something that connected Morris with the man with the bandaged face. But I can't figure out what that could be since Dak Hassan didn't then know Morris and doesn't now seem to know who the man with the bandaged face is. It seems impossible, and yet I have a hazy idea…."

"What?" Biggers asked hopefully.

Daniels shook his head. "No. Not yet. I want to look around here a little… I'll tell you as soon as I find out anything for certain." He made a sudden impatient gesture. "If I only had more time—*time!* But I've got Pete Carson's case to take care of. I've got the evidence here, and I've got to study it and familiarize myself with it. I've only got a day to do that, and that isn't long enough to start even—let alone trying to play detective on the side."

Biggers cleared his throat. "I—I kinda wish you'd concentrate on Pete. I hate to see that kid…" He moved his thick shoulders defensively. "Well, he's a good boy! I like him, and I want to see him get the breaks."

"He'll get them," Daniels promised firmly. And meant it.

THE SUN, BRIGHT and hot in Daniels' face, awakened him, and he turned over in bed, closing his eyes sleepily against its glare.

He had slept late, but his sleep had given him no rest.

He had stayed up almost all the night before, reading the evidence in the case against Pete Carson. The words and phrases of that outline had paraded through his mind in a weary procession the whole night long.

It was, as Jonathan Smythe had warned him, just about as complete and clear and finished and damaging a case as could be imagined. There was no answer to it, and his mind had tired itself seeking one. Slowly now he turned over again and stared at the twin bed under the windows. It was empty. Cora Sue had got up without waking him.

After a while Daniels got up and took a long cold shower that drove some of the weariness out of his mind. He dressed and went into the dining room.

Annie was there, clearing away the dishes.

"Good morning, Annie," Daniels said.

Annie hadn't yet got over her fright. Her pale face was drawn into lugubrious lines, and her colorless eyes kept swiveling around in quick little twitches, as though she expected someone would jump out of a corner at her.

"He's still here," she said, as though it were Daniels' fault. "They didn't arrest him."

"You mean Dr. Morris?" Daniels asked. "They couldn't arrest him, Annie, just because the money-belt and the knife happened to be found on his bed. That's hardly proof of murder."

"Proof enough for me," said Annie. "There's some orange juice in that pitcher. You want your breakfast now?"

"Yes. Some coffee and toast and eggs and bacon, please."

Daniels poured orange juice from the pitcher and sipped at it thoughtfully while Annie went out into the kitchen.

She was back in a surprisingly short time with a sizzling platter of bacon and eggs.

"Annie," Daniels said. "How is it that you are down here at Desert Sands? I thought you stayed up at Phantom Lodge."

"Up there?" said Annie, horrified. "Up there where there's murder been done? I should say not!" She set the platter of eggs down in front of Daniels and leaned closer to him confidentially. "And I ain't gonna stay here, neither, if they don't arrest that Dr. Morris! He'll be murderin' someone else if they don't lock him up!"

"I wouldn't worry about him," said Daniels. "I don't think you're in any danger. Is your husband down here with you?"

"That bum!" said Annie. "Yeah. He's out there in the garage doin' some work or pretendin' he is. You want anything else to eat?"

"No, thanks," said Daniels.

Annie went away again, still muttering that their lives were in danger, and that she, for one, didn't propose to put up with it much longer.

DANIELS ATE HIS breakfast slowly, and then went out through the doors at the end of the dining room onto the terrace in back of the house. It was paved with red brick and beyond it the back lawn was a long rectangle enclosed by the high white wall. There was a swimming pool at the far end.

Pausing on the terrace for a moment, Daniels wondered again at the weather. The sky was a clear, thin blue with a sun like a fat, yellow coin hanging motionless in the middle of it. It was warm without being uncomfortable. The air carried a clear, fresh cleanness, and he breathed in deeply again and again.

He walked down the white gravel path that had segments of lawn, green and square and precise, on each side of it. A sprinkler made a constant, regular flick, flick of sound as it sprayed glittering drops in a never ending circle. The rich desert soil sucked in the water with never-ending voracity.

The swimming pool stretched lengthwise across the back of the lawn, another paved terrace surrounding it. Blair Wiles sat at one corner wrapped in the heavy folds of his blanket. His one eye was closed against the sun, and his scarred face was drawn into a hard, tired knot.

Dr. Morris, lean and elegant in white flannels, lounged in a chair at the other end of the pool.

Cora Sue, in a blue bandeau and trunks and a white bathing cap, was sitting on the edge of the pool dabbling her feet in the water and watching Dak Hassan, who was performing with all the enthusiasm of a trained seal, blowing and puffing, splashing the water into white froth with expertly synchronized arms and legs.

Daniels did not need to be told that all this energy was for Cora Sue's benefit, and a little smile, half contempt, half displeasure, tightened on his face as he strode toward them.

Cora Sue waved a slim, bare arm. "Jim, I thought you'd never get up. I've been waiting for you. The water is marvelous this morning. Put on your bathing suit and come in with us."

Daniels shook his head. "Sorry, dear. I'm busy. You go ahead."

Cora Sue took him at his word. She slipped into the pool

and raced for its other end with Dak Hassan ploughing along gallantly beside her.

Daniels looked back toward where Wiles sat and then nodded thoughtfully at Dr. Morris. "Mr. Wiles doesn't look very happy this morning."

"He drank too much last night," Morris said shortly. "I told him so."

Daniels squatted down on his heels beside Morris' chair. "Just how serious is Wiles' affliction?"

Morris said: "Depends on what you call serious. He was about as badly injured as a man can be. In fact, to be frank, I don't see how I ever pulled him through."

"Is he totally crippled?" Daniels asked.

"No, not totally. He can walk after a fashion if he has some support."

"I've never seen him walk," Daniels said, idly.

"No," said Morris. "He doesn't like to do it where anyone can watch him. It's rather a clumsy procedure. He's sensitive about his appearance. Why all this sudden solicitude about Blair Wiles?"

"Curiosity," said Daniels.

He got up and walked through a gate at the side of the wall. There was a flat space here, and he could see the drive coming up from the road below in a long, looping swing, ending in front of the three-car garage. The garage doors were open now, and Daniels walked slowly toward them.

AS HE CAME closer, he heard a little swishing sound and then saw a man sweeping the garage floor with a long, flat brush. The man was small and fat and pudgy, with mild bluish white eyes that blinked near-sightedly and apologetically at Daniels.

"Are you Bill, Annie's husband?" Daniels asked.

Bill admitted it with a reluctant nod. "Yup."

Daniels stared down at the little pile of sand under the brush.

"How did that get in here?" he inquired. "Aren't the doors tight?"

"They're tight when they're shut," said Bill sullenly. "But somebody went and opened them while we were away and a lot of this sand blew in on the floor."

Daniels looked up at him quickly. "The doors were open? Was anything stolen?"

"Nope," said Bill. "Not a thing. I guess some bum just wanted a place to sleep. The wind gets kinda sharp down here at night, if you're out in the open."

Daniels nodded. He leaned over and picked up a dab of sand from the pile in front of the brush, and rolled it back and forth on his palm. There was just enough oil mixed with the sand to make it stick together in a tight little wad.

"Thanks," he said to Bill. He turned around and walked back across the flat space in front of the garage toward the gate in the wall.

Dr. Morris suddenly appeared through it, and he stopped short when he saw Daniels.

"I didn't think of it before," he said. "I suppose I owe you some thanks for last night."

"Why?" said Daniels.

Morris made an impatient gesture. "That fool of a deputy here might have arrested me and taken me into San Benito. A thing like that doesn't do a doctor's reputation any good."

"Do you care?" asked Daniels.

Morris scowled. "And why shouldn't I?"

"Well, Blair Wiles seems to be your only patient, and I don't think your reputation would bother him much. By the way, have you changed your mind about telling me the identity of the man with the bandaged face?"

"I've told you a dozen times I don't know who he is," Morris snapped.

Daniels held out his hand and opened it fully to show the little wad of packed sand it held. "You see this? This is sand, with just a little oil mixed in it. It came off the garage floor. You remember the sand we found on Mrs. Gregory's window sill? It was just like this. It was stuck together slightly with oil."

"It might have come from any garage floor," Morris said.

"It might have," Daniels admitted, "but I don't think it did. I think it came from this one, and I think the fact that it did explains quite a few things that have been worrying me."

"What things?" Morris demanded.

"It explains how Dak Hassan knew that the man with the bandaged face had some relation with you. When Dak Hassan came up to the Lodge at Phantom Lake, he saw a car parked back of mine in front of the garage. Dak Hassan had hired a taxi to bring him up there.

"When he saw those two cars there, he investigated them. He is just the type that would like to have a little advance information on the guests that were at the Lodge. I know he investigated the cars because I had left a briefcase in mine and it had been tampered with when I came back the next morning. He investigated the other car, the one that was parked back of mine, also. What kind of a car have you, Dr. Morris?"

Morris said: "A brown Packard coupé, if it's any of your business."

Daniels was looking down at the sand in his palm. "Where is it now?"

"In the garage. I had an accident and bent both the front fenders. It's being repaired. I haven't had the time to pick it up."

"Are you *sure* it's in the garage?" Daniels asked.

"Of course I am."

"I DON'T THINK it is, Dr. Morris. I think that car, your brown Packard coupé, was the one that was parked back of mine at Phantom Lake the night Mrs. Gordon was killed. Dak Hassan looked at the registration card. He knew it was your car."

"You're insane," said Morris.

"Perhaps, but I still think your friend with the bandaged face was driving your car that night."

Morris' face was white with fury. "That suggestion is as mad as some of your other accusations. I don't know just what interest you have in all this, Daniels, but I warn you that I am not going to stand for much more of this meddling. My car is in the garage. I do not know the man with the bandaged face. Do you understand?"

Daniels said flatly: "I understand that you're a liar. Dak Hassan saw the man with the bandaged face. Later he learned that the man with the bandaged face used your car to get away from the Lodge.

"You didn't complain about it. From that, Dak Hassan deduced that you knew who he was and had some reason for not saying anything. Dak Hassan has been trying to blackmail you, hasn't he?"

"I suppose, since you're Blair Wiles' guest, I can't prevent you from uttering libelous nonsense like this," Morris said flatly, "but at least I don't have to listen to it. You're a fool, Daniels. A meddling, presumptuous fool. Don't try to ride too far on the prestige of your wife's money. Some people don't have as much regard for it as both you and Dak Hassan seem to."

He turned on his heel without waiting for an answer and strode around toward the front of the house.

Daniels watched him go, frowning a little bit, and then Cora Sue's voice said from behind him, quietly:

"Jim."

Daniels looked back over his shoulder. Cora Sue was standing in the gateway and he knew from the discouraged slump of her shoulders that she had heard what Morris had said to him. She was wearing a woolly white robe and thick-soled bathing slippers now, and she looked like a small child who had been cruelly and unjustly punished.

She came forward a little unsteadily, and touched his arm.

"Jim. Jim, has that money always got to come between us?"

Daniels said: "People will put it there if they can." He opened his palm and dropped the little wad of sand on the ground.

"What was that?" Cora Sue asked.

"Sand," said Daniels. "The same kind of sand I found on Mrs. Gregory's window-sill the night she was murdered. It came from this garage."

Cora Sue's eyes widened slowly, watching him. "You think—"

Daniels shook his head. "I'm not sure yet. Not quite sure." He moved his shoulders uneasily "I'm sorry, dear, I've got to go in now and study Pete Carson's case some more. I haven't much time."

"Jim," said Cora Sue. "Jim—make them sorry for the things they've said about us—about you and my money. Make them sorry."

15

THE JUDGE TAKES OFFENSE

THE COURTHOUSE OF Crater County was a new one and it gave evidence both of the government's liberality and the imagination of its architect. It was a massive, dignified pile of a building with white plaster walls and a red tile roof. The halls were long and straight and spacious with high arched ceilings and cork flooring.

The room in which Pete Carson was to be tried was in the front of the building at the right side. It came closer to resembling a movie set than any courtroom Daniels had ever seen. The spectators' seats were padded with expensive blue plush and the floor under them slanted down a little, giving each row an unobstructed view of the court proper in the front of the room.

When Daniels came through the gate in the railing the spectators' section was already full. Jonathan Smythe had taken up his place at the defense counsel's table. Jonathan Smythe, himself, looked like a man who was about to sit down to a good dinner. His long soberly, mock-solemn face was agleam with perspiration, and good intentions. He nodded exuberantly at Daniels, mopping the top of his bald head with his handkerchief.

"Glad you got here," he greeted. "Everything is ready, and the lambs are prepared for the slaughter."

Daniels had stopped at the end of the counsel's table and was looking at it in dismay. "What's all this?" he demanded.

The table was completely piled from one end to the other with law books, texts and pamphlets.

Jonathan Smythe winked elaborately. "Camouflage. I haven't read any of 'em, but they look pretty good, don't they?"

Daniels pushed some of them away and made an empty space for his brief case at the end of the table. "You finished with the jury selection yesterday?"

"Yeah. We went through it fast. Boken thinks he has a cinch, and he doesn't care who's on the jury."

Daniels had opened his brief case and was taking out some notes he had made on the case. "The jury won't make much difference here."

"What do you think of it now?" Smythe asked, indicating the case notes.

Daniels shook his head. "Bad."

"Well," said Smythe cheerfully, "anyway we've got a crowd. Did you see 'em standing in line outside? There must be three times as many people waiting as this room will hold. I hear some smart guys are standing in line early and then selling their seats. Believe me, brother Daniels, this case has worked up a lot of noise just on account of you and your doings. It's surprising how interesting a little money will make a person.

"Say, what was all that hi-jinks down at Desert Sands last night, anyway?"

Daniels shook his head impatiently. "Later. Is this the district attorney coming now?"

THREE MEN WERE coming through the door at the back of the room beside the judge's stand. The one in the lead had an unmistakable air of congratulatory self-importance. He had black, close-clipped hair, and a forbidding frown. His jaw was pushed out pugnaciously, and he looked as if he was keeping it there with an effort.

He had dressed for the occasion. He wore a brownish tweed suit and a dark brown shirt and tie and his shoes were polished to a gleaming luster. The two men with him were obviously his assistants.

They both had the same weary, hangdog air and were loaded down with case books.

"That's Boken all right," Jonathan Smythe said. "He's putting on his prima donna act."

Boken gestured dramatically to his assistants, sent them stumbling on their way toward the prosecutor's table. Then he whirled around and came up to Daniels and Jonathan Smythe and stopped with a quick sharp click of his heels. "Mr. Daniels? I am Boken, the district attorney."

"How do you do?" said Daniels.

"How do you do?" said Boken. Without another word he whirled with the same military precision and marched back to the prosecutor's table and sat down importantly between his two assistants. He began to shuffle books and papers around.

"He didn't seem to see me," Jonathan Smythe said. "Maybe I'm getting invisible in my old age. And come to think of it, I don't think he approved of you."

"I got that impression," Daniels said.

There was a low drone of muttered conversation among the spectators, and the bare walls picked up the sound and magnified it. It was a warm day, and the sun, bright with the moisture it carried, flooded in long golden streaks through the windows on the south side of the room. The minute hand of the modernistic electric clock over the judge's dais crept around and touched the hour.

The rustling murmur of the audience grew louder and then died away slowly.

The door back of the jury box opened and the jury came in.

Daniels watched them with a sort of curious interest. The whole courtroom was watching them with the same sort of curious and detached interest, and the jury knew it. They were ordinary people, and the same kind of people you see going across any busy street intersection, and they were embarrassed and flustered at this sudden elevation to prominence.

There were seven men and five women, and they sat down in their appointed positions in the jury box with awkward jostling among themselves. They sat down, and then there was nothing else for them to do, and they stared back at the audience with pained half smiles.

Judge Pooley came in through the door that led to his chambers and took his seat on his high dais. The tension in the room heightened.

Daniels looked at the clerk's desk. The clerk was a fat, puffy little man, and he was bent over now tying a shoelace. Daniels jumped up out of his chair and kicked it over backward with a clatter.

"You!" he yelled at Jonathan Smythe. "You! What have

you done?" His voice rode over every sound in the room and brought a dead, awed quiet.

Jonathan Smythe was staring with his mouth open. "W-what?"

"You fool!" Daniels shouted. "You criminal! Is that the jury you selected?"

Jonathan Smythe nodded blankly.

"Why, why—sure."

Daniels strode up to the judge's dais and reaching up on top of it slammed his fist down emphatically in front of Judge Pooley's nose. "I demand that this jury be dismissed!"

Judge Pooley was a scrawny, stooped little man. He had a long, yellowish, thinly twisted face. He looked like he was suffering from stomach trouble. He had dull little eyes streaked with reddish veins, and they goggled grotesquely now.

"What?" he sputtered. "What is this?"

"That jury!" Daniels repeated loudly. "I demand that you dismiss it."

Judge Pooley slumped back into his chair. "Dismiss the jury?" he repeated, incredulously. "Are you insane? What possible reason—"

DANIELS WAVED HIS arms dramatically. "Look! Just look at them! Just look at those twelve faces and picture the narrow, ignorant, prejudiced minds behind them! Look at them sitting there and gloating. Look at them sitting there and slavering and drooling with the thought of torturing and damning a harmless boy who has no chance to fight back! Look at them! Vanity and ignorance and intolerance personified!

"I demand that you dismiss this jury and call a whole new panel."

Daniels' outburst had caught Boken flat-footed. He was standing beside the prosecutor's desk in petrified amazement, staring with his mouth open wide. Now he suddenly came to life. He waved his arms and shouted in a furiously shrill voice: "I protest! I protest! This is an outrage! This is contempt of court!"

Pooley slapped his gavel down on his desk. "Mr. Boken, you be quiet! Mr. Daniels, I have heard of your reputation, but I did not think it would manifest itself in such violent form so soon. This jury has been regularly and properly selected as you well know and is part of this court, and your slanderous accusations are a direct affront upon it, and upon this court. I hold you in contempt and I fine you—"

Daniels' manner had changed completely, and he looked blandly innocent. "Your honor, if I may interrupt for just a second, I would like to point out that this court is not as yet in session. Therefore the words to which you object were not uttered in the presence of the court."

Pooley's breath whistled between his teeth. He leaned down over his dais and glared at the clerk. The clerk spread his hands in an elaborate gesture of agony. "Your honor, I was tying my shoe. I didn't see you come in."

Boken was shouting again: "That is mere subterfuge! The announcement by the clerk is simply a formality! Whether or not it is made has no bearing on whether the court is in session or not!"

Daniels said smoothly: "Perhaps that is so, but may I point out that the court cannot be in session to try the defendant unless the defendant is present? That is his constitutional right."

"The defendant," Pooley echoed, noticing for the first time that Pete Carson was not at the counsel's table. "The *defendant!* Where is he? Where's the sheriff?"

16

THE DEFENSE TAKES EXCEPTION

AS IF THAT were his cue, Sheriff Grimes appeared through the door beside the judge's dais dragging Pete Carson behind him. Grimes had intended to make a dramatic entrance, and he succeeded far beyond his own expectations.

"You call me?" he asked in surprise, looking up at Pooley.

"Yes, I called you!" Pooley answered savagely. "What do you mean by keeping the court waiting this way?"

Grimes' round, red face lost some of its color. "Well— well I just, stopped to get a drink of water—"

"Never mind what you stopped for!" Pooley snapped. "Get the defendant over there at the table where he belongs! This court's time is valuable!"

He gestured angrily.

Grimes' loose lips twisted uncomfortably beneath the ragged yellow of his mustache. Hurriedly he dragged Pete Carson across the floor towards the counsel's table. Pete was handcuffed, and he looked small and shrunken and pitifully woebegone in the grasp of the sheriff.

Grimes slammed him down in the chair beside Daniels and started to fumble with the handcuffs.

Daniels took a hand instantly. "I object to this obviously

staged scene," he said angrily. "It was designed to impress upon the jury that the defendant, here, is a dangerous and vicious character which is obviously not true. I suggest that the sheriff and the district attorney could have improved their act if they had brought in the defendant tied up in a straitjacket and loaded down with leg-irons."

Boken was on his feet. "He can't put that interpretation on the ordinary method of confining a prisoner! This prisoner has already escaped once—"

Daniels interrupted, addressing Judge Pooley: "Your honor, that statement is prejudicial. If the defendant has ever escaped from the custody of officers entrusted with his care, that is a crime and it is so stated plainly in the statutes. It is not at issue in this trial. To bring it before this jury is misconduct on the part of the district attorney. I ask that the jury be dismissed and this declared a mistrial."

Pooley slammed his gavel down on his desk again. "Order! Order in this court!"

Boken was clawing the air. "Your honor! That statement was an aside! It was not spoken to a witness!" He sputtered vainly seeking words, and then ended up in a triumphant tone: "Besides, the court isn't yet in session!"

Pooley's mouth twisted viciously and he leaned forward once again over his desk to glare down at the clerk. The clerk didn't need any added reminders. He began to gabble the stereotyped rigamarole that preceded the court's opening in a high-pitched falsetto. He was so flustered that he twice got mixed up and had to go back and repeat himself. He finally finished up with a triumphant, "Sit down!" and proceeded to follow his own order, popping back into his chair with an exhausted gasp.

Both the bailiff and Judge Pooley were hammering with their gavels, shouting: "Order! Order!"

Daniels was standing in front of the Judge's dais now, and as soon as he could make himself heard, he said: "Your honor. I must insist upon a ruling on my motion. Whether or not the court was in session is immaterial. The district attorney's remarks were made in the pres-

Jim reached a hand into the pool,
afraid of what he might find.

ence of the court and in the presence of this jury. I cite that as misconduct. I demand a mistrial."

"Order!" Pooley said shrilly. "Mr. Daniels, be quiet!" He struck the desk thunderously with his gavel. "Order! I *will* have order in this court! Mr. Daniels, your motion is over-ruled. The remark by Mr. Boken was an aside. It was not made in the due course of this court's procedure."

"I ask an exception," said Daniels.

"Granted," Pooley said shortly. "Now, Mr. Daniels, you

go over there and sit down at your table. Mr. Boken, you be seated. I warn you both that I will not tolerate any further scenes of this nature. You have both been guilty of misconduct that bordered on contempt. Because of the circumstances I will reserve my judgment now, but I warn you both that I will not tolerate such actions in the future."

THE FOREMAN OF the jury was a thin, gaunt man with big ears and a solemn, wind-burned face. He had been holding himself in with obvious difficulty all during the foregoing proceeding, and now he spoke up angrily: "Listen here, your honor, that lawyer fella hasn't got any right to speak about the jury like he did. I ain't slavering and drooling about anything, and I ain't on this jury because I wanta be. They put me here—"

"Silence!" Pooley yelled. "Sit down!"

The foreman shook his head stubbornly. "That lawyer fella ain't got any right to insult—"

Pooley's voice went up to a screech. *"Sit down!* You are in contempt of court!"

The foreman sat down reluctantly, still grumbling.

Pooley glared at him and then at Daniels who was also sitting down now, and then at Boken. He raised his head and eyed the audience but he couldn't find anything to complain about there. The audience wasn't making a sound. Every person was straining forward in his seat listening in tense concentration, trying to follow the course of the argument between Boken and Daniels.

Pooley waited for a moment, breathing hard, and then he said slowly and savagely: "Now—now we will proceed, and there will be no more interruptions. Mr. Daniels, is the defense ready?"

Daniels nodded. "Ready."

"Mr. Boken, is the prosecution prepared?"

"Yes, your Honor," said Boken.

"Well then, go ahead."

Boken made an effort to regain his lost dignity. He got up and paced across the floor to the jury box, pausing on his way to scowl dramatically at Daniels.

"Ladies and gentlemen of the jury," he said smoothly, "You have been selected to try the defendant here, Peter Carson, on the charge of murder in the first degree. The People maintain that on August 17th of the present year, the defendant did strike and brutally beat one Dolly Hyde wantonly and maliciously and with malice afore-thought, so that her death was caused directly as a result. The People will show that the defendant and his victim had been keeping company for some two years before the event." Boken emphasized the words "keeping company" slightly, and then paused in a knowing manner at the end of the sentence.

Daniels had been reading some papers on his desk and he looked up now. "I don't care for the district attorney's insinuation. If he means to show that there was anything improper in the relationship between Peter Carson and Dolly Hyde, he should so state plainly."

"The phrase 'keeping company' seems plain enough to me," said Judge Pooley. "Proceed with your address, Mr. Boken."

"Of course, I didn't mean to insinuate anything improper," Boken said in a voice that indicated that he did. "To aid Mr. Daniels' understanding of the point we will say that Dolly Hyde and Peter Carson had been 'going out' together for a period of some two years previous to her murder.

"We will show that Dolly Hyde's father and her brothers objected to this relationship—rightfully so, it would seem. We will show that they had warned both Dolly Hyde and Peter Carson that the relationship must cease. We will show that this warning was boldly disregarded by Peter Carson, but that Dolly Hyde, in a spirit of filial loyalty, did not disregard it. We will show that she no longer wanted to see Peter Carson and that she told him so. We will show that Peter Carson in a fiendish rage at this perfectly innocent action on her part, did so brutally beat her that her death resulted."

BOKEN NODDED ONCE to show that he had finished, turned around with his customary military precision, and marched back to the prosecution table.

"Mr. Daniels?" said Judge Pooley inquiringly.

Daniels shook his head. "I prefer to wait before I address the jury until I see what further distortion of facts the district attorney proposes to inflict upon it."

"Mr. Daniels!" Pooley shouted. "That is contempt! I will not warn you again! Mr. Boken, call your witness!"

Boken called Dr. Karl Graycil.

It was the first lull in which Jonathan Smythe had the opportunity of talking to Daniels. While the witness was being sworn he leaned close and whispered in Daniels' ear: "When you stir up trouble, boy, you use a big spoon. I expected Pooley to adjourn us to a jail cell any moment."

Daniels shrugged irritably. "Boken was trying to impress me, and I thought I'd beat him to the gun."

Jonathan Smythe grinned. "If they were expecting something fancy they sure got it. You *were* in contempt there at first, weren't you?"

"Yes," Daniels admitted frankly. "Of course. But I was counting on what you said about Pooley. I didn't think he'd be sure enough of whether I was or not to take the chance."

Jonathan Smythe sighed. "Give me a little warning next time, will you? You nearly scared the pants off me."

The witness, Dr. Graycil, looked so much like the traditional conception of a doctor that it was almost unbelievable that he actually was one. He was a wiry, middle aged man with a grey van dyke. He had a gravely intelligent, kindly face, and his eyes peered with a sort of gentle tolerance through silver rimmed pince-nez.

He was a good witness. He talked in a careful, slow voice, and in answer to Boken's questions identified himself as the assistant medical examiner of the county. He also engaged in the private practice of medicine.

Yes, he remembered the date of August 17th of the present year. On that day he had received an emergency call summoning him to the Hyde cottage in Coldiron Canyon. He had left his office immediately and driven to the Canyon as fast as possible.

Arriving there he found Henrietta Parkins waiting in front of the cottage. Miss Parkins was hysterical, and he could obtain no information from her. Going in the kitchen of the cottage, he had found the victim, Dolly Hyde, lying on the floor in a welter of blood.

"How did you identify the victim, doctor?" Boken asked him.

"I had known Dolly Hyde for years," Dr. Graycil said sadly. "I officiated at her birth, and at one time or another during her childhood I treated her for measles and mumps and a broken arm—"

Boken held up his hand. "Thank you, doctor. The question was a formality. You were well acquainted with Dolly Hyde, and you now testify that it was she that you found on the morning of August 17th lying murdered in her father's cottage?"

"I do so testify," said Graycil carefully.

"Did you examine the body of Dolly Hyde at that time?"

"At that time, only superficially. I ascertained that she was dead."

"What was the cause of her death?"

Graycil said: "Her skull was crushed by repeated heavy blows from some blunt instrument."

"Did you perform an autopsy on the body?"

Graycil nodded. "Yes."

"Did you ascertain the heavy blows that you spoke of were the sole cause of Dolly Hyde's death?"

"I did," said Graycil.

"There was no possibility that she died from other cause or causes?"

"None whatsoever," said Graycil positively. "Dolly Hyde was an exceptionally healthy girl. The blows and nothing else caused her death."

"Thank you, doctor," said Boken. "Your witness, Mr. Daniels."

Daniels shook his head. "No questions."

As Dr. Graycil left the stand, Jonathan Smythe nudged Daniels and whispered: "You were smart to leave the old boy alone. The Doc is a square shooter, and everybody in town knows it."

Daniels nodded absently, watching Boken's next witness take the stand.

THE WITNESS, GEORGE BITTENDORF, identified himself as a deputy-sheriff of Crater County. He was a heavy-set little man with a pouter-pigeon chest. He sat up importantly in the witness chair, trying to make the most of his height. He had a hard, square-jawed face; and he kept his lips in a thin, disapproving line as he watched Daniels and Pete Carson with suspiciously narrowed eyes.

"Do you remember the date, August 17th of this present year?" Boken asked him.

Bittendorf nodded with emphatic precision. "I do."

"Describe what happened on that date."

Bittendorf took a firmer grasp on the arms of the chair. "I was on duty at the sheriff's station here at San Benito, that afternoon. A telephone call came in, and I took it. It was Henrietta Parkins. She said something terrible had happened at the Hyde cottage in Coldiron Canyon and to send somebody out there at once."

"Did you do that?" Boken inquired.

Bittendorf nodded again in his positive way. "I went out myself. The two sheriff's patrol cars that are assigned to this area were over at Holden at the Rodeo taking care of the traffic."

"And what happened on your arrival?"

"This Henrietta Parkins was waiting for me in front of the house, and she flagged me down. She said that Dolly Hyde had been murdered."

Daniels said: "Objection! That's hearsay."

"It's not offered as direct testimony," Boken protested,

"but merely to show the reason for the officer's subsequent action."

"Overruled," said Pooley. "Go on, Mr. Boken."

Boken nodded to Bittendorf. "You stated that you found Miss Henrietta Parkins in front of the Hyde residence and that she told you that Dolly Hyde had been murdered. What did you do then?"

"I ran right into the house," Bittendorf said, in a tone that indicated that he thought that this was a pretty brave thing to do. "I ran into the kitchen and I found Dr. Graycil there examining Dolly Hyde's body."

"What happened then?" Boken asked.

"Dr. Graycil told me that Miss Parkins had called him before she called me. He told me that he had examined Dolly Hyde and that she was dead, and her death was the result of repeated blows on her head with some heavy instrument."

"And then?" Boken inquired.

"I made an investigation," Bittendorf said complacently. "I looked the whole place over."

"Did you find the murder weapon?"

"Nope. I couldn't find it anywhere. I searched the whole house, and then I went out in front and talked to Miss Parkins. She told me that she saw Pete Carson running—"

Daniels got up on his feet this time. "I object to that testimony. It is hearsay, and is offered in direct evidence. Miss Parkins made the statement at a time when the defendant was not present, when she was not subject to cross-examination, and when she was not under oath."

"The objection is sustained," Pooley said sourly. "The

witness will confine himself to those things that he knows of his own knowledge."

Boken shrugged. "All right, Mr. Bittendorf. What did you do next?"

"I went over to Miss Parkins' house and called back to the station. I told them to send out a radio car to pick up Pete Carson, but the deputy told me that he already had been caught—"

"Objection!" said Daniels sharply. "That's hearsay again."

"All right, all right," Boken said irritably. "Let it go. Now Mr. Bittendorf, let us go back for just a second in your testimony. You stated that when you came into the kitchen you found Dr. Graycil examining Dolly Hyde's body. Where was the body lying?"

"At the side of the room, halfway under a little breakfast table. I asked Dr. Graycil if he had moved it, and he said that he had not. She was lying on her face, and the back of her head had been smashed in, and there was blood all over the floor."

"Thank you, Mr. Bittendorf," Boken said in a satisfied tone. "That will be all. Your witness, Mr. Daniels."

Jonathan Smythe grimaced at Daniels warningly. "Watch out for this guy," he muttered. "He's one of Boken's stooges. He'll harpoon us if he can."

DANIELS GOT UP from the table. With his head down and his hands folded behind him he paced back and forth in front of the witness stand. He took three or four turns and then stopped about ten feet away. He said, without looking at Bittendorf: "What's your name?"

Boken had been watching like a cat. "Objection!" he said

triumphantly. "The question is repetitious. The answer is already in the records."

Daniels looked up, surprised. "Doesn't the witness know his own name?"

Pooley said: "The question is repetitious but not objectionable on that ground. Get on with it, Mr. Daniels."

Daniels looked at the witness. "Well?"

Bittendorf was scowling. "My name is George Bittendorf."

Daniels took three, long pouncing steps, toward him, suddenly shot out his hand and pointed his forefinger squarely at Bittendorf's nose. "Spell it!" he shouted.

Bittendorf jerked back in the chair, surprised. "Huh? Why, it's—it's—B-i-t-t—"

"Hah!" said Daniels, without waiting for him to finish. "You can't even spell your own name!"

"Objection!" Boken shouted. "Objection!"

Daniels swung around savagely, "On what grounds?"

Boken appealed to Pooley. "He's trying to intimidate the witness. That question is irrelevant and immaterial and has no bearing."

"So!" said Daniels. "The fact that the witness is so stupid that he can't even spell his own name is immaterial? I don't think it is. I think it's very material."

Pooley hammered his gavel on the desk, and Bittendorf yelled angrily: "I can so spell my name! It's B-i-t-t-e-n-d-o-r-f!"

"Well, well!" said Daniels sarcastically. "So you're really able to spell your own name! That makes you a very clever fellow. Do you think you could add up to four without counting on your fingers?"

"Objection!" Boken chanted. "Objection! Objection! That's not proper cross-examination! He's attempting to intimidate and confuse the witness!"

Pooley pounded vigorously with his gavel. "Mr. Daniels, I have warned you for the last time. You are in contempt of this court and I fine you the sum of fifty dollars."

Daniels closed his eyes in martyred resignation. He reached in his pocket and brought out a dollar bill. It was crumpled and indescribably dirty and one corner had been torn raggedly off.

"Your honor, this is the defendant's money. It is all the money he has. He was saving it to buy cigarettes and candy and a magazine or two. Little things, true, but very precious to a man who has lost his freedom. However, I have no choice.

I will use it to pay this fine, adding, of course, the proper amount of money of my own."

Pete Carson was staring at the bill in wide-eyed incredulous wonder as Daniels carefully straightened it out between his fingers.

THE GAUNT JURY foreman spoke up again: "Say, listen, your honor, I don't like to see that kid deprived of his last dollar, just because that lawyer of his don't have very good sense. I'll chip in a dollar for him."

Another member of the jury, an elderly comfortable-looking woman, in the back row added, nodding accusingly at Daniels: "Young man, you have no right to take that poor boy's last dollar. You give it right back to him."

Pooley's gavel made a thunderous frenzy of sound that echoed deafeningly from the walls. "Silence! Silence! Both of you be quiet! Order in this court!" He glared down at Daniels, breathing hard and trying to control his voice "Mr. Daniels, I am not at all sure that these last words of yours have not been an aggravation of your previous contempt. However, under the circumstances I will suspend the fine. But I warn you that its sum will be added to any future fine if you again disturb the orderly process of this court."

"Thank you, your honor," Daniels said meekly. "I will try to restrain myself."

"I would advise it," Pooley said ominously. "Have you any further questions to ask this witness?"

"None," said Daniels.

Pooley looked over his shoulder at the clock. He turned back and nodded at the clerk. "The court is recessed until two o'clock this afternoon." He gathered his robes around him and disappeared through the door into his chambers.

The audience suddenly broke into an uproar and half a dozen reporters and photographers jammed the gate in the bronze railing trying to push their way through, shouting demands and questions at Daniels.

"You take care of them," Daniels said to Smythe.

"And how!" said Smythe.

Daniels patted Pete Carson comfortingly on the shoulder and worked his way through the press toward the rear of the courtroom. He went through the door opposite to the one used by the jury, through a short corridor, and then down one of the long, high halls that led toward the rear of the courthouse and the parking lot there. As he reached the door, there was a hesitantly cautious hiss behind him.

It was Biggers. The deputy-sheriff nodded meaningly to

Daniels and then pulled him behind the shelter of a half open closet door.

"You did swell," he murmured. "You sure kept them birds jumping. Have you found out anything new about that deal down at Desert Sands?"

"A little," said Daniels. "I've found out what kind of a car the man with the bandaged face is or *was* driving. It's a brown Packard coupé, a new one. It belongs to Dr. Morris. That's how Dak Hassan connected Dr. Morris with the man with the bandaged face. Dak Hassan saw the car the night of Mrs. Gregory's murder. He knew that the man with the bandaged face used it to get away."

"Ho!" said Biggers in pleased surprise. "So that's the way it was!"

Daniels nodded. "Morris claims the car is in the garage, but I'm sure it isn't. You can easily find out the license number and broadcast a pick up order on it. You'd better issue a 'Go slow' order along with it because I don't think the man with the bandaged face will come in without a fight."

"He'll come in feet first if he tries that," Biggers said. "I'll get at it right away."

17

THE JUDGE TAKES A REST

DANIELS GOT BACK into court a few minutes before two. Jonathan Smythe was there ahead of him, sitting at the defense counsel's table with a big pair of horn-rimmed glasses on the end of his nose, gravely perusing a thick lawbook. He put it down with a sigh of relief when Daniels appeared.

"This fine print hurts my eyes," he remarked disgustedly. "I never could read cases or look up references. Maybe that's why I'm not much good as a lawyer." He beamed suddenly, cheering up. "But I'm sure good at suggesting headlines to reporters. Wait till you see the big blow that comes out in the papers tonight, I was very mysterious about the course of action we intend to take in the future. That was very easy because it's as big a mystery to me as it is to anyone else."

"To me, too," Daniels admitted frankly. "It just depends on what happens."

"Not that I like to appear too dumb," said Jonathan Smythe, "But just what was the idea of ribbing the jury the way you did this morning? You don't think that's going to make them pals of yours, do you?"

Daniels shook his head impatiently. "No, of course not. I wanted to make them dislike me. The more so the better."

"Well, why?" Jonathan Smythe asked blankly.

"So they'll sympathize with Pete, of course. I want them to think that I am a hot-tempered, loud-mouthed crackpot. Then they'll be sorry, for the poor kid's neck depends on me. The more I annoy them, the more they'll sympathize with him and lean over backward to give him every possible break. It's obvious that what I do isn't his fault."

"Oh," said Smythe, chewing his under-lip thoughtfully. "Well, why not try to make them friendly toward you?"

Daniels smiled grimly, "I'd like to, but it wouldn't work. In the first place I'm a stranger coming in here to take this case with a big hullaballoo, and in the second place there is the little matter of my wife's money. It has been getting a lot of advertising."

Jonathan Smythe stared shrewdly at him, "That must get you kinda down."

"It does," Daniels said shortly, "And now for the moment I'd like to forget it."

"Oh, sure," said Jonathan Smythe, "Sorry. You see this crowd here? It's the same bunch that was here this morning. I don't believe a one of 'em went out to get lunch. They knew they wouldn't get their seats back if they did. Looks like we're havin' bank night."

BOKEN AND HIS two assistants appeared. Pointedly ignoring Daniels and Smythe, they sat down at the prosecution table and began whispering in a three-cornered conference.

The jury came in, a little more certain of themselves now, a little less embarrassed. They were already becoming accustomed to the procedure of the court and to their own roles in it. Two attendants were patrolling the aisle between the spectators' seats, constantly on the lookout for any violation of the court's dignity.

Sheriff Grimes brought in Pete Carson, and Judge Pooley took his place on his dais. The clerk called the court to order.

Boken called Gerald Cragen. Cragen was a small, dry, precise little man who looked as if the whole proceeding was distasteful to him. He spoke in an indifferent monotone. In answer to Boken's questions he identified himself as a scientific criminologist.

Jonathan Smythe took time out to nudge Daniels and whisper: "This guy is good. Damned good. A national authority in his field."

Daniels nodded silently.

Cragen testified that on the afternoon of August 17 he had been called by the sheriff's office and requested to take his equipment and proceed to the Hyde cottage in Cold-iron Canyon. He had done so.

"And what did you find on your arrival?" Boken asked.

Cragen said in his bored, slightly disapproving tone: "I found County-detective Bittendorf in charge. He conducted me to the kitchen. Then I found Dr. Graycil and the body of the deceased."

"Did you examine the body?"

"Yes. I did so at Dr. Graycil's request."

"Please inform the jury of your findings."

Cragen turned his head slightly toward the jury, "I found, in accordance with Dr. Graycil's diagnosis, that the deceased had met her death through the agency of repeated and heavy blows upon the back of her skull. The skull was shattered badly, bits of bone matter being driven into the brain."

Boken said: "Did you find the instrument that inflicted these blows?"

"No. Detective Bittendorf informed me that he had searched the premises, but I instituted a careful search of my own. There was no agency in the house or in its vicinity which could have inflicted those wounds."

"Could you form an opinion of what kind of a weapon it was?"

Cragen moved his shoulders slightly. "Not very adequately. It was a long, round instrument, blunt and quite heavy, judging from the force of the blows."

Boken went back of the prosecutor's table and returned to the witness stand with a large stiff piece of paper possibly a yard square. He presented it to Cragen with a dramatic gesture. "Now, Mr. Cragen, to make your subsequent testimony clear to the jury, I wish you would observe this map. Do you recognize the room it portrays?"

Cragen nodded indifferently. "Yes. It is a map of the kitchen of the Hyde cottage in Coldiron Canyon."

"You testify that this is a true and accurate map of that kitchen?"

"I do," said Cragen.

Boken turned to Pooley. "The People submit this map as People's Exhibit A."

Pooley looked up. "Mr. Daniels, do you wish to examine this map?"

"No thank you," said Daniels.

THE CLERK MARKED the map, and it was passed around among the jury and returned to Boken, who held it up at an angle so both the jury and Cragen could see it. "Now, Mr. Cragen, in reference to this map, just where was the body found, or rather just where was the body when you saw it?"

"Under the kitchen table at the side of the room. Dr. Graycil told me that it had not been moved since its discovery."

Boken marked a spot on the map with his pencil. "This square represents the table to which the witness is referring," he explained to the jury. "In what position was the body lying when you saw it, Mr. Cragen?"

"The head, shoulders and half of the torso were under the table, the feet and legs extending out on the kitchen floor."

"From that position could you deduce how the deceased was standing when she was so murderously struck down from behind?"

"I would say that she was standing with her back to the kitchen table, possibly two or three feet away."

"I refer you again to the map," Boken said. "Is there anything else besides the table and its chairs on this side of the room?"

"Nothing else."

"No windows?" Boken inquired.

"Not near the table."

"Then," said Boken, with knowing emphasis, "from that, you deduce that the assailant was seated at the table?"

"Objection," Daniels said. "That calls for an opinion and conclusion on the part of the witness."

"Sustained," said Pooley.

Boken wasn't displeased. He nodded in a satisfied way

at the jury. "He could have been seated at the table, Mr. Cragen?"

"He could have been," Cragen said.

"And there is no other reason for him to have been in that particular place, is there?"

"Objection," said Daniels again. "Same grounds."

"Sustained," said Pooley.

"All right," said Boken amiably. "We will drop that for the moment and consider the rest of the room. You examined it carefully, Mr. Cragen?"

"For the sake of the records." Daniels said, "that is a leading question and objectionable."

"Yes, yes," Boken said mockingly. "Of course, Mr. Daniels. Consider it withdrawn. I will try again. Mr. Cragen, did you examine the room?"

"I did," Cragen said, obviously bored.

"Tell the jury what you found, making reference to the map, here."

Cragen said: "The body was found as I have previously described. The table under which it lay was partially set, that is, there was silverware on it and three plates. There were three cups and saucers. One cup and one saucer were on the floor, shattered. The table was a little out of line, not quite flush with the marks on the floor that indicated where its legs usually were set. There was a smear of blood on the top on one side, the side toward the main part of the kitchen."

"What conclusions do you draw from these observations concerning the table?" Boken asked.

Cragen moved his shoulders in a slight distasteful shrug.

"That the deceased, when she was falling, struck the table and jarred it."

Boken turned around. "Any objection. Mr. Daniels?"

"No objection," said Daniels calmly.

Boken rubbed his hands. "I am so glad that this meets with your approval. Now, Mr. Cragen, tell us what else you found."

"There was a partially prepared meal on the stove, a coffee percolator, a frying pan with some meat in it, and a pot with some beans in it. The beans and the coffee had boiled dry and the meat was burned to a cinder."

"All right," said Boken. "What did you do next?"

"I examined the premises for fingerprints."

Boken's eyes glistened eagerly. "Did you find any?"

Cragen nodded. "Yes. I found prints on the table, the chairs, the doors, the stove and on the linoleum beside the point where the body was lying."

"Have you identified these fingerprints?"

"I have. I took impressions from the fingers of Dr. Graycil, from Miss Henrietta Parkins, from Detective Bittendorf and from the fingers of the deceased, and found all these prints present at various points in the room."

Boken paused for a full ten seconds and then he turned his head slowly to glare accusingly at Pete Carson. "And Mr. Cragen—did you find any other prints?"

"I did," said Cragen.

"Did you identify those other prints?"

"I did."

"And to whom do they belong?"

"They are identical with those of the defendant, Peter Carson."

Boken whirled around. "And do you object to that, Mr. Daniels?"

"Of course not," said Daniels, "We don't have the slightest intention of denying that Pete Carson visited the Hyde cottage very often. You made that statement yourself in your opening address to the jury."

BOKEN LOOKED AS if he suddenly had a bad taste in his mouth. He marched over to the prosecution table and came back with a sheaf of enlarged photographs in his hand. "Mr. Cragen, look at these. Are they the photographs of the defendant, Peter Carson, that you found in the kitchen of the Hyde cottage?"

"They are."

"And examine these others. Are they fingerprints of the defendant taken by you after his apprehension?"

"They are."

Boken said: "I submit these as People's Exhibit B."

"Mr. Daniels?" said Pooley.

Daniels moved his hands lazily. "Not interested."

"You will be!" Boken snapped. He took the photographs away from the clerk and distributed them to the jury who passed them around among themselves, staring at them with uncomprehending awe.

"Now, Mr. Cragen," said Boken, "tell the jury where you found the fingerprints of Peter Carson in the Hyde kitchen."

"On the door," said Cragen precisely. "On the table, on the linoleum beside the body and on a polished brass buckle that the deceased wore around her waist on a braided leather belt."

"On the body," Boken said, nodding meaningly to the

jury. "On the body itself." He went marching back to the prosecution table, leaned over, and with the air of a magician, suddenly jerked his hand high over his head holding a wide, braided leather belt. It shivered and jerked as realistically as a live thing in his grasp.

Beside him Daniels heard Pete Carson draw in a sudden sobbing intake of breath. His voice was a choked murmur. "I—I give Dolly that—"

Boken was watching in sly anticipation, holding the belt out and waving it back and forth in front of him.

Daniels moved his elbow slightly, and one of the big case books on the table toppled off on the floor with a thunderous bang. At the same instant Jonathan Smythe began to cough. He coughed so loudly and agonizingly that the whole room rang with the echoes of it.

Judge Pooley banged his gavel for order.

Jonathan Smythe recovered himself and apologized in a wheezing gasp.

Boken strode forward angrily. "That outbreak was staged purposely to distract attention from my actions!" he accused.

"Yeah?" said Jonathan Smythe, still red in the face. "Let's see you cough that way on purpose."

"Order!" Pooley shouted. "Mr. Smythe, your apologies are accepted this time. Mr. Boken, proceed with the questioning of your witness."

Boken went back to the witness stand, still scowling. He showed the belt to Cragen. "Is this the belt to which you referred, Mr. Cragen, the belt on the buckle of which you found the fingerprints of the defendant, Peter Carson?"

"That is the one," Cragen said.

"Let the jury understand you clearly.

The deceased was wearing this belt, and the fingerprints of the defendant were found upon the buckle?"

"That is correct," said Cragen.

"And that is all," said Boken gleefully. "Mr. Daniels, do you wish to question the witness?"

Daniels yawned realistically. "No, no questions."

Judge Pooley was looking over his shoulder at the clock. "It is nearly time to close this session, Mr. Boken. I don't believe that it would be profitable to start the examination of another witness now. The court will adjourn until tomorrow morning at ten o'clock." He went through the door into his chambers as the clerk was making the announcement.

"Mr. Daniels," Pete Carson said in a low apologetic mumble. "I—I'm sorry I busted out like that—I didn't mean to, but it come so sudden—and I—I give Dolly that belt. I braided it for her myself, and she was—was so proud of it. When I seen it—it just—"

Daniels touched his arm. "I know, boy. It doesn't matter. Boken did it on purpose. He was hoping that you'd make some break that he could capitalize on before the jury." He nodded to Jonathan Smythe. "And that was a mighty quick pickup on your part."

Smythe grinned. "I'm gettin' smarter every day, only I'll have to think up something else next time. My throat feels like I swallowed a quart of gravel after that last session."

Grimes took Pete Carson in custody and hustled him out the rear door of the courtroom.

Jonathan Smythe watched him go, his eyes squinted

up in a worried little frown. "This afternoon wasn't so hot, huh?"

"No," Daniels admitted.

"That fingerprint stuff is going to be mighty tough to get around."

"Mighty tough," Daniels agreed. "It made a big impression on the jury, but there was no use in any cross-questioning. The man was an expert, and he knew what he was talking about. Cross-questioning would just have served to emphasize the evidence in the jury's mind."

"Yeah," said Jonathan Smythe. "Looks like you're going to have to shake some tricks out of your sleeve mighty quick."

"I've got a couple in mind," said Daniels, hoping grimly that he sounded more confident than he felt. "I'll see you tomorrow morning."

18

THE CORPSE TAKES A DIVE

DANIELS WAS STILL driving the little sedan that he had hired the day he had arrived in California. Its engine gurgled and muttered as he swung it up around the steep curve of Blair Wiles' driveway. He parked it at one side of the space in front of the garage and got out, retrieving his bulging briefcase from the back seat.

It was dark, a soft smooth velvet darkness that was like a soothing bandage laid across the smarting tiredness of his eyes. Below him the canyon was a narrow, darkly impenetrable slot that opened out gradually, wider and wider until it became the valley that housed the town of Desert Sands. The town itself lay like an outspread hand down on the desert floor, a glittering cluster of varicolored lights that moved and twinkled in silent distant laughter.

Daniels stood there looking down at it and drinking in the restful quiet of the night until he heard the low smooth tinkle of a piano from somewhere close to him. The notes hung in the air like individual round jewels incredibly and hauntingly sad. Daniels followed the sound through the gate in the wall and found that it came from the living room that opened out onto the terrace.

There was light behind the long windows and Daniels

stopped on the terrace to peer through them. The room was all in shadow except for one drop-light over the grand piano in the far corner.

Foley was playing it with a sort of dreamy aimlessness. He was playing beautifully, and Daniels recognized the piece as something of Beethoven's. He pushed back one of the windows and entered.

Foley looked back over his shoulder and nodded at him. "Hi, keed. I hear you've been having a busy day." The music went on, effortless and rippling.

Daniels had advanced far enough now to see Mrs. Foley, and he stopped in surprise, watching her. She had a big towel spread out on the floor, and she was lying on her stomach on top of it. She was resting her chin in one hand. The other held a pencil with which she was making zigzag marks on a sheet of yellow paper. She was wearing a skimpy white bathing suit, and it made her look like a scrawny little girl with frizzed yellow hair and a drawn tired face. She didn't pay any attention to Daniels.

"What's all this?" Daniels asked, indicating her with a nod.

Foley played on without breaking the rhythm of the music.

"Timing a gag," he explained absently. He was wearing a fuzzy yellow bathrobe that was wrapped tight around him.

"Timing?" Daniels repeated blankly.

"Yeah. That's the best half of a gag. It's got to come off just at the right second. Otherwise it lays an egg." He jerked his head to indicate his wife. "She does the timing while I furnish the sound effects."

"Play faster," Mrs. Foley ordered.

Foley obediently stepped up the tempo of the piece. "Pour me a drink, will you?" he requested of Daniels, nodding toward a pitcher and glass sitting on a tray on top of the piano.

Daniels put his brief case in a chair, and picked up the pitcher. He was amazed to find that it contained ice water.

"Are you really going to drink this?" he asked Foley.

Foley winked at him. "This is Thursday. I never drink liquor on Thursday. Don't ask me why. I don't know. It's just an old custom in the Foley family."

Daniels handed him the glass of ice water. Foley drank it with his left hand, still playing the piano with his right.

"I'd like to talk to you." Daniels told him.

Foley looked down at his wife. "Hey, how about it?"

"Nuts," said Mrs. Foley. She put the pencil down and rolled over on her back, cradling her head in her hands and staring disapprovingly up at Daniels. "Why didn't you either come sooner or later? Now I've got to do this whole thing all over again."

"I'm sorry," said Daniels, "but this is rather important."

"So is our pay check," said Mrs. Foley. "And millions of fans will cry in their beer if Milt Merton doesn't get his next comedy out in time."

"Never mind her." Foley advised Daniels, "She's got a hangover. What do you want?"

"DO YOU REMEMBER talking to me day before yesterday in the bar at the hotel in San Benito?"

"No," said Foley. "Did I?"

"Yes."

Foley scratched his head. "How drunk was I?"

"Very. You passed out while you were talking."

"That accounts for it, then. What was I talking to you about?"

"About the man with the bandaged face. You said you knew who he was."

"Well, well," said Foley wonderingly. "Can you imagine that?"

Daniels held on to his patience. "Do you know who he is now?"

"No," Foley admitted. "Haven't the faintest idea. I never can remember things I do when I'm drunk. It's a handy habit to have. No regrets in the morning."

"Could you remember if you were drunk?"

Foley pursed his lips judicially. "Well, maybe."

"Go get drunk, then," said Daniels. "I want to know. It's vitally important."

"Get drunk?" Foley repeated. "Me? Oh, no. Not on Thursday."

Daniels' voice had a sudden rasp to it. "Don't you realize that the whole investigation is stopped completely by just that one thing? We don't know who the man with the bandaged face is. We can't go any further with the case until we know."

Foley looked at his wife again. "How about it, kid? Shall we break our rule? It's in the interests of justice and higher things of life?"

Mrs. Foley sat up and clasped her bare arms around her knees. "Oh, all right. I suppose we might as well."

Foley played a dramatic chord on the piano. "Hurray! Onward and upward!"

"Do you have a house here?" Daniels asked.

Foley nodded. "Oh, sure. Just across the canyon. We

don't have a swimming pool, though, so we came over here tonight to take a dip and then decided to do a little work while we were here. This piano is a lot better than mine, anyway. Wiles keeps it in tune."

"Where are Wiles and the rest of them?" Daniels asked.

"This is Thursday," Foley explained.

"I know that," said Daniels, "but what of it?"

Foley shrugged. "Thursday night is servants' night out— an old California custom. Blair Wiles and the rest went hunting some food. I imagine they're down at the Glades. That's a night club at the other end of the valley. It has a neon sign about fifty feet high. You can see it from the terrace, if you want to go and look for them."

Daniels said: "No, I don't think I will. I ate on the way down here, and I've got to study up on some of my case notes."

"You've cut yourself out a piece of work," Foley commented. "Looks to me like they've got that kid all sewed up."

"Not yet, they haven't," said Daniels.

Mrs. Foley got up, picked up her towel and wrapped it around her thin waist like a sarong. "Well, come on, dummy, if you're coming."

She went out through the French windows onto the terrace and Foley shambled after her with a casual wave of his hand.

DANIELS STARED AFTER them, scowling a little. They were such an incredible pair that it was hard to believe they were real. He wondered if Foley actually knew who the man with the bandaged face was, or if that was just a drunken hallucination, or if the whole thing had a meaning that was far more sinister.

Foley, to all intents and purposes, whether drunk or sober, seemed harmless enough; but Daniels had reached the point where he was beginning to doubt his own observation and judgment. The whole business was insane, and Daniels dismissed it from his mind with an annoyed shrug.

Certainly there was nothing more he could do about it for the moment.

He pulled a chair up under the lamp and opened his briefcase. Taking out the notes he had scribbled that day at the trial, he began to shuffle them over with a wearily dogged persistence. It was only by an unbelievable effort that he could concentrate. Even one day of trial work seemed to drain all his mental energy.

He was tired with an inert, leaden tiredness that dragged at him like clutching hands, drawing his mind down into the soft comfort of sleep. He fought the weariness back again and again, but it was too strong, too heavy, and the scribbled lines of his notes began to blur in front of his eyes.

He slept uneasily, and the testimony he had heard at the trial that day kept running through his mind in disconnected snatches. He was hazily conscious of the other voices before he realized that they were not part of his dreams. Then he sat up with a startled jerk that snapped him awake like the shock of cold water.

He stared around him, tense and alert. He was alone, sitting in the big chair under the lamp, but the voices were still there. They were low voices, faintly muffled and the words they spoke were undistinguishable, but there was a crackling anger in their tones.

After a second Daniels located the direction from which they were coming. On the way out the Foleys had left one of the French windows open, and the voices were coming from the darkened yard outside the house. Two men were talking, and one of them was Dr. Morris. Daniels did not recognize the other voice, but there was something about it that raised a little instinctive aversion deep inside him.

He got out of the chair and walked toward the open window very slowly and quietly, keeping against the wall out of sight from the yard. He pulled a corner of the drape aside, feeling the cool stir of air in his face, and peered out. His eyes were accustomed to the light inside, and he could see nothing. But the voices were much plainer, and Dr. Morris spoke out in a sudden wild flare of anger:

"Trying to involve me in your mess, you damned fool!"

The other voice said in a thin drawl, "It isn't my mess, but you're in it with me. Getting a little fancy, weren't you? Weren't satisfied with half of it—you wanted it all."

"I had nothing to do with it!" Morris said. "Do you think I'm insane?"

"No, just smart. But not smart enough. You saw a nice chance to pull that job and flop it right in my lap, but I'm not taking it. You come across with that dough—all of it."

"I haven't got it!" Morris said. "Will you please understand that! *I haven't got it!* I never saw it!"

"All right, Doc, if that's the way you want it."

THERE WAS A queerly tense silence then while Daniels peered out from behind the drapes, shading his eyes.

Morris and the other man were down near the swimming pool. Daniels could make out their shadowy forms without being able to distinguish one from the other, and then Morris said, with a sort of incredulous contempt:

"Put that gun away. Do you think you can scare me? *Me?*"

The other man didn't answer, and Daniels could feel a crawling tensity in the air.

Morris' voice suddenly went high and shrill with fear: "Put that gun down!"

Daniels swept the drapes aside and stepped through the window. His heel clicked on the paving of the terrace, and the sound suddenly ripped the dead silence into a thousand pieces.

Down by the swimming pool there was a quick, deadly swirl of movement. A revolver report made a dull blast of sound. Morris cried out frantically, and his cry was swallowed up by a sullen splash of the water in the swimming pool. Only one shadowy figure was there now, crouched a little, facing Daniels.

Daniels dodged sideways instinctively. There was a sudden spit of orange flame from in front of the shadowy figure. The night echoed again to the blast of revolver fire, and the bullet smashed the pane out of a window at Daniels' right. Gravel crunched as the shadowy figure ran diagonally across the yard. It reached the gate, fumbled with it, and then was through. The gate slammed thunderously shut behind.

Daniels ran that way, and he was almost to the gate when water splashed in the swimming pool again and there was a choked gurgle of sound that could only have been a feeble appeal for help.

Daniels checked himself in mid-stride and turned that

way. He knelt down on the edge of the pool and tile was cold and slick and wet under his hand. The water was like a sheet of crumpled cellophane, glittering greenly, and in its depths he saw the distorted moving fingers of a hand groping upward blindly.

Daniels went down flat on his stomach and reached. His hand touched the groping fingers, and they slid wetly away from him.

He crawled further over the edge of the pool and lunged down again. This time he caught the soggy edge of a sleeve. He hauled back, scrambling for purchase on the smooth tile, and then the surface of the water broke apart, and he was staring down into the agonized, grotesquely twisted face of Dr. Morris. Morris' lips were moving, and the water was red where it touched them.

Daniels got to his knees, changed his grip to Dr. Morris' coat collar.

He jerked, bracing himself firmly, and pulled Morris up over the edge of the pool. Behind him the water made a little gurgle of disappointment. Morris squirmed weakly on the edge of the pool, his right arm held up toward Daniels. His lips moved. He was trying to get words out, but no sound came, and then his arm fell limply down, and his palm hit the tile with a little smacking sound.

"Morris!" said Daniels urgently. "Dr. Morris!"

Morris didn't answer and didn't move.

His eyes were wide and glassy and lifeless, staring up into Daniels'.

19

DANIELS TAKES A BOW

DANIELS STRAIGHTENED UP. He looked toward the gate and took a step that way indecisively, and then inside the house the telephone started to ring with an abrupt, shrill violence.

Daniels hesitated for a split-second longer and then ran the length of the yard, across the terrace and through the French window. He swept the telephone up from its stand.

"Hello," he said breathlessly. "Hello!"

"Greetings and salutations, my legally learned friend," said Foley. "I have a message of some minor importance to impart to you. Do you recall the subject of our discussion and the reason for my noble experiment in the interest of science? Well, astounding as it may seem, in view of the circumstances, I have achieved success."

"What?" said Daniels. "You remembered who the man with the bandaged face is?"

"I remembered," Foley confirmed. "You see, I found when I came back here to my domicile, that I had nothing to drink but some particularly bad Scotch. Particularly bad Scotch reminded me of a certain bar which shall remain nameless in the city of San Benito. However, although their Scotch is bad, the bar happens to be convenient. It is near the post office.

"After considering this matter for a sufficient length of time, I recalled that I had stopped at the bar in question on the day in question. Therefore I had visited the post office either before or after, because I wouldn't stop at that bar if I hadn't. So then it became clear.

"I remembered that I had seen our friend with the bandaged face at the post office. He was hanging on the wall of that edifice."

"Hanging on the wall?" Daniels repeated incredulously.

"Right," said Foley. "Not in person, of course, but his picture was on the wall."

Daniels drew in his breath sharply. "You mean—a reward poster?"

"Right," said Foley. "Our friend's name is Charles Raker, and the government would like to have him explain the robbery of three mail trucks and the murder of a postal guard. Mr. Raker, by the way, is also wanted by the State of California for a little matter of bank robbery and two murders. You see he's by the way of being a public enemy. Not a very big public enemy, of course, but then if he works hard and saves his money, perhaps he will eventually reach a place of prominence in his chosen field."

Daniels had not even listened to the last part of this discourse. He was staring blankly at the wall in front of him, and now he reached out gropingly and closed the connection on the telephone. As though it had been waiting that opportunity, the instrument rang instantly again, trembling with its shrill eagerness.

Daniels lifted his hand. "Yes?" he said absently.

It was Biggers, the deputy sheriff, and he was wildly excited. "Daniels? Listen here. You were right about Morris' car. It wasn't in the garage. A guy came and got it out about four days ago. The garage owner didn't know him, but the guy had a letter from Dr. Morris, and he paid for the job in cash, so the garage man let the car go. It was picked up today abandoned over in Dole County. Just on an off chance I had it checked for fingerprints and I found 'em. Boy! I found 'em! I know who the man with the bandaged face is!"

Daniels said slowly: "Is his name Charles Raker?"

"Huh!" said Biggers, deflating with a sudden gasp. "How—how in hell did you know that?"

"Foley told me. He seems to have a remarkable memory for features. He saw the man with the bandaged face at Phantom Lake the night Mrs. Gregory was murdered, and he told me then that he thought he had seen the man's eyes somewhere else. He called me and told me that he had seen them on one of the reward posters in the post office."

"Well I'll be damned," said Biggers blankly. "But look here! Now we got it! Now we can put the squeeze on Doc Morris. He's been aiding and hiding a fugitive from justice and when we start pushing that charge he's going to have to open up!"

His voice had grown stronger and triumphant as he spoke.

"No," said Daniels slowly. "No. Morris won't do any more talking, ever. Raker shot and killed him tonight. You'd better come right down here."

THERE WAS A long, smooth sweep of lawn in front of the courthouse, and it was dotted with excitedly talking little clusters of spectators, when Daniels arrived the next morning. He pushed his way through the crowd on the front steps into the hall of the courthouse before he was recognized. The hall was packed, and three reporters lurking just inside the door spotted him simultaneously. They made for him, shouting questions, and flashlight bulbs popped their brilliant flares.

The whole massed crowd in the hall surged and heaved, trying to get closer, trying to see, trying to hear. Daniels was helpless in the crush until two attendants pushed their way through to him and fought the crowd back. Behind their interference, Daniels slipped into the courtroom. Every seat was taken and there were more attendants on guard at the door, refusing to allow any more to enter.

Daniels went down the aisle, and a curious excited mutter from the audience seemed to gather behind him and follow him.

Daniels realized that the strain must be telling on him now, because those voices sounded remote; they seemed to be partly muffled by the dull ache in his brain. Yet somehow, he knew, he had to clear his thinking in the next few minutes.

Jonathan Smythe was waiting for him at the gate in the railing. "Whooey!" he said in relief, "I was afraid you wouldn't make it."

"I almost didn't," Daniels said.

"You're sure stirring things up," Jonathan Smythe said. "Another murder, and now a public enemy! The papers are going crazy. I guess they'll have to stop those wars in China and Spain until we git through here. There's not room enough to print all the news about you and them both."

Daniels put his brief case down on the counsel's table and took out his handkerchief. He wiped his forehead. His hand was trembling a little, and Jonathan Smythe saw it.

"Whoa!" he said alarmed. "Don't let go now! *I* can't hold this together! The ship will sink right under us!"

Daniels face was white and set with strain. "I won't let go," he promised. "But I can't take much more of this. I feel like a man on a nightmare merry-go-round, it keeps going faster and faster and faster, and I can't get off and I can't stop it. I don't know what to do."

For an instant, then, he felt his self-control slipping; his own words seemed to make it vividly clear to him how helpless he was. But with an effort of will he managed to get hold of himself, and he looked up to find Smythe staring at him. Daniels forced a grin.

"Just try this case," said Jonathan Smythe. "Just try this case. That's all."

The court was called to order and for his first witness, Boken summoned Henrietta Parkins. She was thin and waspish and had scanty grey hair drawn up tight in a knot on top of her head. Her eyes were watery blue behind thick-lensed rimless glasses. She had a long, narrow face and tightly set lips.

She came through the gate in the railing at a fussy half-trot. When she came even with the defense counsel's table she stopped short and threw her hands high in an awkwardly horrified gesture.

"There he is!" she shrieked in a high falsetto. "There's the murderer of that poor helpless girl!"

The courtroom drew its breath with a collective gasp.

Daniels was sitting beside Pete Carson, partially in front

of him. He jumped up out of his chair and said: "I'm sorry madam, but you've made a mistake. I am not the defendant here. I am his attorney." He whirled around and stared toward the judge's dais. "I want to register a most emphatic protest against this clumsy effort on the part of the district attorney to influence the jury. It is obvious that the witness was coached to put on this scene, but the coaching was so clumsy that she mistook me for the defendant!"

"That's a lie!" Boken yelled. "A lie! She was referring to Pete Carson! She was looking right at him!"

"So!" said Daniels. "You admit you coached her!"

"I do not!" Boken yelled. "That's slander! I protest!"

He was on his feet, and his broad face was deeply flushed; his lips were working with anger.

Judge Pooley was pounding unavailingly with his gavel. "Silence! Silence! Order in this court!"

20

THE WITNESS TAKES THE STAND

BOKEN WAS SHOUTING over the noise in the room: "Your honor, your honor! I protest against the slanderously criminal accusation made by the attorney for the defense! I did *not* coach the witness! She was temporarily overcome by the horror of coming face to face with the defendant again. The remarks were uttered as a result of momentary hysteria!"

Daniels said: "She certainly isn't a very reliable witness if her hysteria results in such confusion even before she starts to testify."

"Mr. Daniels!" Pooley shouted, "Your remarks and your conduct are in contempt of the dignity of this court! I fine you the sum of one hundred dollars!"

"That won't bother him much," Boken said in a barely audible tone. "His wife has plenty of money."

A muscle in Daniels' face twitched. He was white with restrained fury, and he controlled his voice with an effort that shook him. "Mr. Boken, won't you repeat that remark in a louder tone? I don't think everyone here heard you."

Boken backed up a step, raising one arm in an awkward half-gesture of defense.

"Mr. Daniels," Pooley said. "Mr. Daniels! I impose an additional fine of fifty dollars!"

Daniels turned his head slowly to look at him. He didn't say anything, but his expression was so eloquently savage that Pooley's face lost a little of its color.

"Thank you," said Daniels in a low voice. "Thank you, your honor."

Pooley moistened his lips. "You may pay the fine to the clerk at the end of this session."

"I shall do so," said Daniels. He sat down in his chair, and the tension that had gripped the room relaxed slightly.

There was a rustling murmur from the audience, and the clerk rapped sharply for order. Henrietta Parkins was sworn, and sat down in the witness chair. Boken had lost his air of confidence. He made a visible effort to regain it, but his voice shook a little as he asked the first formal question.

Henrietta Parkins had an air of righteous indignation. Yes, she snapped, she certainly did remember the day of August 17th. She would, in fact, never forget it as long as she lived.

"Tell the jury in your own words what happened on that day." Boken requested.

HENRIETTA PARKINS TURNED and faced the jury with an important little bustle. It was obvious that she was going to enjoy this. Her watery eyes glistened eagerly behind the thick lenses of her spectacles.

"I was washing that day. I always wash twice a week. I say a body can't keep things proper and clean just washing once a week.

"The Hyde cottage is about a hundred yards further up

the Canyon than mine. I can see it from my back porch where I wash. I could see that poor, dear girl working and scrubbing around the house."

Henrietta Parkins paused to dab gingerly at her cheeks with a wadded handkerchief.

"Please try to control yourself, Miss Parkins," Boken said. "I realize that this is a great strain on you."

"It is," Henrietta Parkins agreed tearfully. "Oh, it is!" She drew a deep tremulous breath and went on bravely: "After a while, as I was rinsing my clothes, I saw a little smoke coming out of the chimney of the Hyde cottage. I knew that Dolly had started to get supper for her dear, brave father and brother. A little later I went outside to throw away my rinse water, and then I smelled something burning."

She paused to nod tragically at the jury. "Little did I realize the awful thing that was happening, but I thought it was queer because Dolly was such a good, industrious little girl and such a fine cook. I had never known her to burn anything before, so I stood there on the back steps watching, and it was the will of Providence that I did, because I saw the murderer!"

"Yes?" said Boken eagerly. "Yes? Who did you see?"

"Peter Carson!" Henrietta Parkins spat the name out as though it were a loathsome thing.

"What did you see him doing?"

"He was running away from the back door of the Hyde cottage, running and stumbling and falling, and looking back over his shoulder. His face was all twisted up like he was crazy."

A hush blanketed the courtroom as the millionaire's
wheelchair jerked two paces nearer Daniels.

"Thank you, Miss Parkins," Boken said. "Thank you for your bravery in testifying to this horrible matter."

Henrietta Parkins closed her eyes. "It was my duty," she said dramatically.

"Your witness, Mr. Daniels," Boken said.

Daniels stood up. He picked up a pamphlet from the table in front of him and held it up, opening it at random. "Read this, Miss Parkins," he requested.

"Now I protest," Boken said. "It's obvious that no person with normal eyesight can read that fine print at that distance."

Daniels said smoothly: "Miss Parkins does not have normal eyesight. She has phenomenal eyesight. She can see through the walls of a house a hundred yards away. Compared to a feat like that, reading print at this distance should be very easy."

"She never testified to that," Boken snapped.

"Oh yes, she did, by implication. She said that she saw the murderer, whom she identified as my client. How about that, Miss Parkins? You did say that Pete Carson was the murderer, did you not?"

"I certainly did!" said Henrietta Parkins with an emphatic nod. "He is!"

"Did you see him commit the murder?"

"I saw him running away."

"Answer my question Miss Parkins. Did you see Pete Carson commit the murder?"

"Well—no. But I know he did it."

"That's interesting," said Daniels. "How do you know?"

"I saw him running away—"

"That's it," said Daniels. "Now Miss Parkins, the district attorney left you on your own back steps. What did you do after that? After you had seen Pete Carson running away?"

"WELL—I WONDERED WHAT had happened. I kept smelling the burning food stronger and stronger and I thought there was something mighty suspicious about the way Pete Carson was acting. So after he had gone I walked down to the Hyde cottage and around to the back door. I called Dolly's name and when she didn't answer, I rapped on the door. It was kinda half open and when I rapped on it, it opened further and I could see inside the kitchen."

"So?" said Daniels. "And what did you see?"

Miss Parkins shivered realistically. "I saw that poor, poor girl stretched out on the floor and all the blood—"

"Yes?" said Daniels. "And then what did you do?"

"I—I screamed—and then I turned around and ran—"

Daniels interrupted sharply: "Ah! You ran! You ran away! But you just got through telling me that you knew Pete

Carson committed the murder because he ran away. If that is the basis on which we are to judge a person's guilt of murder, then there is just as much reason to believe that *you* are guilty of murder. Did *you* murder Dolly Hyde, Miss Parkins?"

Miss Parkins screamed shrilly and flopped over sideways in the witness chair. An attendant came running with a glass of water.

Boken shouted: "I object to this brutal intimidation of my witnesses!"

Half the audience was standing up, trying to see, and Judge Pooley's gavel thundered out a command for order.

"You needn't worry," Daniels said to Boken. "I have no more questions to ask this witness, but it seems very strange that a person who is glib about accusing other people of murder, exhibits such distress when she, herself, is accused."

"Order!" Pooley shouted. "Mr. Daniels, sit down! The attendant will remove the witness. Silence in this court!"

Henrietta Parkins was removed from the room, sobbing hysterically, and Boken summoned for his next witness Constable Ham Grey.

Ham Grey was as round as a ball and he walked to the witness stand with a decided waddle. He had a pinkish hairless face and small wide-set blue eyes with a humorous twinkle in them. He identified himself as the police force of Petersville, which was, in turn, identified as a wide space in the road occupied by a general store, a couple of pool halls, a beer tavern and several oil stations, two miles north of Coldiron Canyon.

Boken said: "I direct your attention to the date of August 17th of this present year. Do you recall the date?"

"Yup," said Ham Grey. "Sure do."

"Tell the jury what occurred on that day."

"Well," said Grey comfortably. "I was sittin' on the bench in front of old man Meekin's general store. It was a right hot day and I was just a-sittin' and a-lookin' and not thinkin' about much but maybe goin' and havin' a bottle of beer for myself, when I heard this voice a-hootin' and a-hollerin' down the road."

"What did you do then?" Boken asked.

"Well—I sorta got up and looked around."

"Did you locate the owner of the voice."

"Yup. I seen Pete Carson a-comin' larrupin' down the road a-yellin' and a-hollerin' fit to kill."

"What did you do then?"

"Well, I couldn't hardly figure it out. Pete, he looked somethin' terrible with his face all twisted up and white and yellin' like he was. I woulda thought maybe he'd tooken himself too much to drink only I know'd Pete never drank nothin' at all, so I up and hollered to him and says: 'Hi, Pete! What's ailin' you anyway?'"

"And what did the defendant answer?" Boken pressed.

"Well, I couldn't hardly make head nor tail of it. He said somethin' about Dolly Hyde bein' murdered up to her house, and I thought maybe he was just jokin'. But then I see he had some blood on his hand and on the knees of his overalls, and so I thought it was maybe serious. And I says, 'Pete, you just better trot along with me now, while we go into old man Meekin's store and give a ring to the sheriff and see what's what!'"

"And then?" said Boken.

"Well, it was like that. We went into the store, and I

rung the sheriff, and he said that there had been a murder reported up at the Hyde cabin, and that they was lookin' for Pete Carson. So I said that I had him."

"You saw the blood on Peter Carson, the defendant's clothes and on his hands?"

"Sure did," said Ham Grey reluctantly.

"You are certain that it was blood?"

"Sure am," said Ham Grey. "Seen a lot of it in my day."

BOKEN WENT BACK to his table and returned carrying a wrapped bundle of cloth. He unwrapped it, taking his time and heightening the suspense as much as he could. He uncovered an old pair of coveralls and held them up in front of Ham Grey.

"Are these the clothes Peter Carson was wearing on the day in question?"

"Sure are," said Ham Grey.

"People's exhibit C," said Boken. He held the coveralls up before the jury. "Ladies and gentlemen, I call your attention to these stains on the knees."

The coveralls were clean, and the stains on the knees were obvious—great dark smears, and the jury goggled at them in horror.

Boken turned toward Daniels. "If the defense wishes, we will offer proof that these stains are blood and were fresh stains on the day in question."

"Stipulated," said Daniels quietly.

Boken blinked and looked a little surprised. He handed the coveralls to the jury and said to Daniels, "No more questions. Your witness."

Daniels got up and nodded in a friendly way to Ham Grey.

Ham Grey nodded back and said: "Howdy."

"Howdy," Daniels answered. "Mr. Grey, have you known the defendant long?"

"Sure enough," said Ham Grey. "Known him ever since he wore three-cornered pants."

"Like him?" Daniels asked.

"Shucks, yes."

"Did you ever arrest him before the time in question?"

"Pete?" said Ham Grey, surprised. "I should say not. Why should I wanta arrest him for?"

"I'm sure I don't know," Daniels answered. "Did you know Dolly Hyde?"

"Yup," said Ham Grey. "Nice girl."

"Do you know her father and brother?"

"Yup."

"Have you ever arrested them?"

"Objection!" Boken said sharply. "There was no proper foundation for that question. The subject was not touched in the direct examination."

"Objection sustained," said Judge Pooley.

Daniels shrugged easily. "No more questions."

Ham Grey was dismissed from the witness stand, and the court adjourned for the noon recess.

21

THE COURT TAKES A REST

BOKEN HAD WORKED carefully, building his case bit by bit, one piece of cold, inescapable fact after the other, enclosing Pete Carson in a mesh from which no artifice could extricate him, and like many another better workman, he had saved his best and most dramatic piece until the last. He was ready to use it now.

At the beginning of the afternoon session he called Pappy Hyde. Pappy Hyde had prepared himself for the occasion. He was spruce and clean, and his scanty brown hair was slicked down over the bald spot on top of his head. He wore an ill-fitting blue suit that was obviously new, but there was nothing that could take the expression of wolfish, hard leanness out of his features or conceal the malevolent glitter in his dusty little eyes.

His two sons were present to back him up, sitting in the front row of the spectators' seats. Their faces had a bitterly savage likeness and they stared at Pete Carson and Daniels with unwavering scowls.

Pappy Hyde's given name, it appeared, was Ranse. He was sworn, and in answer to Boken's careful question, identified himself as the father of the victim.

"Do you know the defendant, Peter Carson?" Boken asked.

Pappy Hyde's lips curled away from his yellowish teeth. "I do."

"What was the occasion of your acquaintanceship with him?"

"He was tryin' to keep company with my daughter."

"And did you object to that?"

"Sure did," said Pappy Hyde bitterly.

"Why did you object?"

"Ain't havin' no dirty rat like that in my family."

"Was Pete Carson aware of your aversion to him?"

Pappy Hyde nodded violently. "You bet he was. I told him so myself. I told him to keep away from my daughter. So did my boys. We told him that we didn't want to catch him around our house no more."

"Tell us why you objected to his attentions to your daughter."

Pappy Hyde glared at Pete Carson. "He's been talkin' loose about her and spreadin' scandal. He ain't no good. He's a loafer and a bum, and always was. I didn't want her havin' no truck with him at all. I told her about him, and she promised me she wouldn't never see him no more."

"Do you know if she ever did see him after you had told her not to and she promised she wouldn't?" Boken asked.

"She seen him once," Pappy Hyde snarled. "When he killed her!"

Boken held up his hand quickly. "But other than that, Mr. Hyde?"

Pappy Hyde shrugged his thin shoulders. "Dolly was a good girl. She wouldn't do what her pa told her not to.

She was kind-hearted, though, and she didn't want to hurt nobody's feelin's—not even his."

"How long before the date of her murder did you forbid her to see the defendant?"

"Couple months," said Pappy Hyde. "Couple months or maybe more."

"Did she feel badly when you told her?"

"Pretty bad," Pappy Hyde answered. "She was just a young girl, and she didn't know nothin' about such fellas as he is. When I told her she cried some, but she wouldn't do anything I told her not to. She understood I was only lookin' out for what was best for her."

"You said that you spoke to the defendant about the same matter. Did he exhibit any signs of anger over your decisions?"

"Huh!" said Pappy Hyde contemptuously. "Him? I should say not. He was scared to. He might come sneakin' around and try and soft-soap Dolly, but he was a-scared to talk to us."

"Did the defendant, to your positive knowledge, ever try to talk to your daughter after you had forbidden him to?"

"Yeah," said Pappy Hyde. "Two days before he killed her, I come home early, and I found him there a-talkin' to her. He was a-yellin' and talkin' mad to her, and she was cryin'. I chased him, but he seen me comin' too quick, and he got away from me."

"Did you exchange any words with the defendant at that time?"

"Not nothin' but swear words," Pappy Hyde said. "He shook his fist and swore at me when he was runnin' away."

"Now, Mr. Hyde," said Boken, "let me summarize your

testimony for the benefit of the jury. If I am incorrect in any matter, please correct me. You, as the father of Dolly Hyde, had certain objections to the attentions Peter Carson was paying your daughter. You so informed him and forbade him to attempt to see her. You also forbade your daughter to see him further.

"Your daughter was willing to abide by your wishes in the matter, but Peter Carson evidently was not. He tried to see your daughter subsequently, and when he was discovered he exhibited bitter anger and resentment against you. And further than that he exhibited anger against your daughter by abiding by your decision. Is that correct?"

"It sure is correct," Pappy Hyde said. "He was a-scared to come back at us, so he come back at her, and it wasn't none of her fault at all." Pappy Hyde got up out of the witness chair and extended a rigid, trembling arm straight at Pete Carson. "But you're gonna pay for it! You hear that? You're gonna pay!"

Pete Carson's face was white and twisted and scared, staring back at him.

JUDGE POOLEY BANGED his gavel for order, and two attendants hurried forward and seized Pappy Hyde and led him out the back door of the courtroom, still struggling vainly in their arms.

"The People rest!" said Boken in a loudly dramatic voice.

Judge Pooley said: "Mr. Daniels, if the defense wishes to question the witness, I will declare a recess until he has sufficiently recovered himself."

Daniels shook his head. "The defense has no questions, but since the defense did not anticipate that the prosecution would close its case so abruptly, we are not fully prepared at this moment. I would like to request an adjournment until tomorrow morning."

Pooley looked at Boken. "Mr. Boken?"

Boken shrugged elaborately. "The defense never will be prepared, but we have no objection to an adjournment."

"So ordered," said Pooley.

In the uproar that accompanied the closing of the court, Jonathan Smythe leaned close and murmured in Daniels' ear. "That put a large nail in the coffin. Why didn't you cross-examine him? A lot of that stuff was phoney as hell. You could have tripped him up."

Daniels shook his head. "No. Not that way."

"What are you going to do tomorrow?" Smythe asked.

"Put Pete on the stand and let him sink or swim by his own story."

"He'll sink," Jonathan Smythe said gloomily, "like a rock."

"Perhaps," Daniels admitted. "But it's the one thing we can do. And tomorrow I want you to have the two Hyde brothers and Pappy Hyde sitting in the front row of this courtroom."

"They'll be there," said Jonathan Smythe grimly. "They'll be there with bells on. I'll see to that little matter personally. What happens if they are?"

"I'm going to put on a little entertainment especially for their benefit," Daniels said.

22

FOLEY TAKES A LOOK

IT WAS NOT yet dusk when Daniels drove the old sedan up the steep slant of the driveway and parked it in front of the three-car garage, but the sun was close to the mountaintops and the blue haze lay close in the bottom of the valley, distorting all that it touched and giving it a queer, pleasant fuzziness. There was no stir of life from any of the other houses along the canyon. The silence was a strange, invisible weight over everything, and Daniels wondered at it vaguely as his feet crunched in the gravel of the drive.

He pushed back the gate in the wall and stared straight into Cora Sue's white, strained face. She was standing rigid in the center of the terrace, and when she saw Daniels she gave an audible gasp of relief.

"Oh, Jim!"

Daniels was tired and sick with the strain of the trial, and with the bitter, beaten feeling of failure, and the sight of Cora Sue there waiting for him was a refreshing thing that seemed to wash away the hard lump of discouragement in his throat. She was suddenly nearer and dearer to him than she had ever been before, and he took her in his arms and held her close.

Her voice came muffled a little against his shoulder.

"Jim, they're having some championship tennis matches today down at the club and all the others went down to see them. I guess everyone along the canyon went, but I wanted to stay and wait for you."

"Thank you for that, dear," Daniels said. He felt her tremble a little, pressed against him and he released her and pushed her back, his hands on her slim shoulders. "What's the matter?"

Cora Sue was trying to smile, but the smile twisted and quivered on her soft lips. "Jim. I'm—I'm afraid. I'm terribly afraid—I rode downtown with the others when they went and then walked back, and there's no one around anywhere. There's—no noise." She made a helpless little gesture. "I'm afraid, Jim—afraid…"

Daniels said comfortingly: "You shouldn't have waited here for me, dear. You got to thinking about Morris and what happened here last night, and naturally that's enough to make anyone afraid."

Cora Sue's voice was taut. "It isn't that. It's something else. It's something here right now. Jim, Annie and Bill aren't anywhere around. They didn't say they were going away, but when I came back I called and called and they didn't answer—"

"Probably went for a walk," Daniels said. "Come, let's go inside. You'll feel better in there."

"No!" said Cora Sue sharply.

Daniels stared at her puzzled. "But why not?"

"I don't know—there's—there's something in there—"

Daniels took her arm. "You come on. All this business has given you a bad attack of nerves, and I don't blame you a bit. We'll go in and play the radio or something, and then you'll feel much better."

She went with him reluctantly across the terrace and in through the big French windows. The low living-room was shadowed and dim and comfortable looking.

"You see?" said Daniels, smiling down comfortingly at her, "There's nothing in here—" His voice died in a little hiss of expelled breath.

"Nothing but me," said another voice, finishing his sentence.

THE MAN WAS standing in the doorway across the room. Standing quite still, with an alert tenseness. He was not large and he wore a dark blue suit and a dark hat with the brim pulled down low over his eyes. His face was pink, a queer light pink like rubber, and there were no lines in it at all. It looked like a mask only it was not a mask. But the thing that Daniels noticed was his eyes—sharp, beady and malevolent. No wonder they were so recognizable that Foley had been able to spot them, even in a photo.

"Raker!" said Daniels. "The man with the bandaged face!"

"Yes," said Raker. "Stand still, both of you."

He had a stubby revolver in his right hand, and he came closer to them now with quick cat-like strides, his eyes never wavering, never blinking.

"What do you want?" Daniels demanded.

"I'm going out of here," Raker said. "I'm taking your wife with me. Now get this. I've got it figured right. I'll hole up for one day with her. I won't hurt her a bit, if you do what I tell you. You get in touch with her old man and tell him to have the Feds pulled off the border, so I can get through. As soon as I get past that border, I'll let her go."

"You're a fool," said Daniels. "A.J. Bancroft can't call off the Federal men."

"He can," said Raker. "He's got a hundred million dollars, and anybody with that many millions can do anything. I tell you, it's the only way I can get out!"

His voice wavered some on the last word and Daniels knew that the man's nerves were tied up into a tight, jittering knot of fear, that he was half hysterical with strain, and that he was all the more dangerous because he was.

Daniels let go of Cora Sue's arm and shook his head slowly.

"It *will* work!" said Raker. "It had *better* work!"

"No," said Daniels. His voice sounded dull and thick in his own ears. "No. You're not taking Cora Sue."

Watching him, Raker raised his stubby revolver until the barrel pointed straight at Daniels' face.

"You're not going to take her," Daniels said in the same dull, desperate voice.

The hammer of the revolver clicked lightly.

"Jim!" Cora Sue said in a breathless gasp.

Daniels suddenly dove at Raker's legs, and he knew even as he did it that it was a foolish and futile thing to do. It was a thing that wouldn't work, that would never work, not with a man as desperate and as quick as Raker. It was a thing that only movie heroes could do successfully.

And then while he was still in the air, hurtling forward, there was a world-filling blast of sound that seemed to strike him and hurl him, flattened and breathless, against the floor. There was no pain, but there was a terrible lassitude that held him, and he couldn't move and couldn't think. Dimly far away he heard Cora Sue scream and then scream again.

He got up without ever remembering getting up or ever remembering how long he had been lying on the floor. The room was empty, and Daniels walked across it like a man in a dream. His feet were leaden clods and he could not lift them. They shuffled along the thick rug, raising little ridges ahead of them.

HE CAME TO the front door. It was partially opened, and he went through it. He didn't remember the step down, just outside, and he fell on his face and gravel cut the palms of his hands. He got up again very slowly and laboriously and he saw Cora Sue and Raker going down the path toward the main road in the canyon. Raker had one hand clamped tightly over Cora Sue's mouth, and he was dragging her along beside him.

"Raker," said Daniels.

Raker whirled around, whirling Cora Sue with him, and looked back up the path. Daniels was coming, one step after the other, still dragging his leaden feet in the gravel.

"Raker," he said.

Raker had Cora Sue held in front of him like a shield, and he was pointing the stubby revolver over her shoulder. His voice was thin and high with fear:

"Get back there! Get back!"

Daniels plodded on toward him, wincing with the effort of each step. He saw the muzzle of the revolver quiver a little and then steady. He knew Raker was going to shoot in the next split-second and that he would not miss. He knew that he could never reach Raker, but he kept on, plodding, plodding…

There was a quick, flat burst of sound from the floor of the canyon. Just that one sound and no more, and then Raker stepped back away from Cora Sue. He raised his hand in a little fumbling gesture toward his temple, and then he turned and fell, sprawling full length on the path with his arm spread out in front of him.

Cora Sue seemed much closer to Daniels. He reached out one wavering arm and his fingers touched her shoulder. "Cora Sue!" he said, and then he knew he was falling and he couldn't stop.

… A little later he came wavering up out of the darkness of the mist, and he could see and think clearly for measured seconds. He was lying on his back. Cora Sue's face, all trembling and smeared with tears was close above his. There was another face, too. Mike Riley's face, with her eyes staring in wide, unbelieving awe.

"If I hadn't seen it—" Mike Riley was saying in a slow, incredulous wonder "—him walking right into that gun." Mike Riley was holding a gun herself. It was a long, slim .22 target pistol. "Lucky I kept this," she said absently. "I was going to pawn it, but it used to belong to my dad, and he taught me how to shoot with it, knocking tin cans off the corral fence. I had it in the car, and when I saw you and that man I ran down and got it—"

THE BLACK CURTAIN snapped down over Daniels' mind again. When he regained consciousness the second time, he was lying on the couch in the living room of Blair Wiles' house. Cora Sue's face was still there, white and anxious, and Mike Riley's, too. There was a third face—a man's face, grave and professional looking. The man's hands were working on the spot of fiery pain that centered high on Daniels' right shoulder. He was speaking to Cora Sue:

"That'll fix it. Not serious, Mrs. Daniels. Not serious at all. But it came damned close. The bullet hit him on the top of the shoulder and nicked a piece out of his collar bone. It didn't miss his spine very far. It must have been a terrific shock. I don't see how he ever got up and walked afterward."

"He walked, all right," said Mike Riley. "You should have seen him."

"Jim," said Cora Sue quickly, seeing his eyes open.

The mists were clearing away, and Daniels smiled up at her. "Is everything—all right?"

Cora Sue squeezed his hand. "All right, dear."

Daniels' eyes sought Mike Riley. "It was—you?"

Mike Riley nodded silently, embarrassed.

There was someone else pushing forward, and then Biggers' earnest perspiring face peered anxiously at Daniels.

"You all right, boy? Is he okay, doc?"

The doctor stood up. "Yes. No excitement, now. No moving around for awhile."

"It was Raker, all right," Biggers said, nodding eagerly to Daniels. "And him with a brand new face, too. He just got it in time to be buried with it. He's deader than a kippered herring. That bullet was only a .22, but you don't need any bigger one if you git it right in the temple." He glanced admiringly at Mike Riley. "That was some shooting, lady. Over fifty yards with a .22. I'd hate to try it."

"My dad spent a lot of time teaching me to shoot," Mike Riley said.

"He sure done a good job," said Biggers. He rubbed his hands, winking at Daniels. "We got things kinda tied up now, huh? There'll be a lot of newspaper boys down here pretty quick. Could you sort of give me the outline?"

Daniels' whole body felt heavy and weak and helpless, but his mind moved with a sharp, quick clarity. He said: "I can tell you a lot of it. I'm sure it's right, but you can check it up later.

"Morris had been hiding Raker, while Raker recovered from an operation Morris had performed on his face. Mrs. Gregory brought that $100,000 out here for Raker. That was his getaway money. But he didn't get it. Someone killed Mrs. Gregory and stole the money. Raker found her dead at the Phantom Lake Lodge that night, and he found that she had been stabbed with Morris' hunting knife.

"Later he found her money belt hidden some place that incriminated Morris further. Morris knew that Mrs. Gregory was going to bring that money to Raker, and naturally Raker thought that Morris had killed her and stolen the money. He put the money belt and the knife on Morris' bed then, to show Morris that he knew Morris was doublecrossing him. Actually Morris was not. He didn't know anything about the money or the murder.

"But Raker was desperate and terror-stricken, crazy to get away from here. He knew he would be caught if he stayed. Morris couldn't persuade him that he didn't know anything about it, and the other night, when I interrupted them, and Morris tried to tackle Raker, Raker killed him."

Biggers looked blankly dismayed. "But—but that leaves us still in the hole."

"I know that," said Daniels. He was silent for a moment,

thinking. "You know, the reason why this isn't all clear to us now is because there's a part of this pattern that is missing. There's a part that has never been in the pattern from the very first. That's why we can't see it. If we could only find that part…" He squinted absently at the ceiling. "There's one thing that has kept bothering me from the first. It keeps prodding and prodding at my mind, and there's no sense to it really but it's always there. Tell me, were there any witnesses to Blair Wiles' accident?"

Biggers nodded blankly. "Yeah. One."

"I'd like to talk to that witness just to get it out of my mind."

"Why, you *can't* talk to her."

"Why not."

"The witness is dead. She was Dolly Hyde."

DANIELS BLEW OUT his breath in a long sigh, and he was smiling. "That's it. That's the missing part of the pattern. I could feel all the time that there was some connection between Pete Carson's trial and this house. It was something deep and hidden, something underlying, and I was right!"

Cora Sue's voice was small and tight with horrified comprehension. "Jim—Jim—you don't think that Blair Wiles—"

"No," said Daniels. "No, of course not. It couldn't have been Blair Wiles. Don't you see? That's the answer."

"Oh," said Cora Sue. "I—I—I don't see, Jim. Who—who is the murderer?"

Daniels said slowly. "It's a man you never heard of, dear. A man named Randall, And now all I have to do is to prove it." He sighed lengthily. "But let that go for the moment.

Mike Riley—I can't even begin to express my thanks for what you did for Cora Sue and me."

Mike Riley shrugged uneasily.

Daniels said: "It's none of my business of course, and you certainly did arrive at just the right time, but I can't understand why you didn't come down here sooner. I told you that Dak Hassan was down here or was coming down. I expected you to come a couple of days ago."

Mike Riley's voice was suddenly bitter. "I guess you might as well know now as later. I'm a liar."

"A liar?" Cora Sue repeated blankly.

Mike Riley nodded once. "Yes. The reason I didn't come down here sooner is because I didn't have any money. Dak Hassan borrowed the last fifty dollars I had. I had to sell my aeroplane—it's just an old box kite tied together with bailing wire—before I could get money enough to come down here."

"But—but—you told Dak Hassan—a million dollars—"

Mike Riley made an abrupt gesture. "I know I did. That's why I'm a liar. I was trying to make an impression on him. I thought a million dollars would. All I had in the world was that old aeroplane and an old broken-down cattle-ranch without any cattle on it.

"I do have a little credit through my father's friends, and Dak Hassan is so nice and sleek and polite—and he has that title—and I thought we could start a dude ranch for society people near Reno. I thought Dak Hassan, being in society himself, and being a prince, rich people would come there… And then—and then—Oh, hell! I love him, darn it!"

"Why I think that's a wonderful idea," Cora Sue said.

There was a sudden altercation at the door and as though

he had timed his entrance to the split second, Dak Hassan burst into the room.

"My dear lady!" he said to Cora Sue.

"My dear, dear lady! I have just heard of your horrible experience, and my heart bleeds—" He saw Mike Riley then, and for the first time since Daniels had known him, he lost his dapperly insolent air. "You!"

"Yes," said Daniels. "Meet your future wife!"

"Her?" said Dak Hassan. "Marry her? Me? Never!"

"Well," said Daniels, judicially. "Of course, you have an alternative. You can go to jail for petty theft, although I think serving a sentence for petty theft would be a little wearing both on your title and on your social position, if any."

"Petty theft?" Dak Hassan repeated. "What are you talking about?"

"You stole fifty dollars from Mike Riley."

"It's a lie!" Dak Hassan shouted.

Daniels moved his one good arm casually. "All right, if you want to be defiant, but I think I must warn you that the jury when they get an inkling of your reputation will be much more likely to believe Mike Riley's story than yours. But there is no use arguing. Better take him away, Biggers."

"With pleasure," said Biggers.

"Wait!" said Dak Hassan, quickly. "Wait, please! A Dak Hassan in jail for petty theft? The thing is preposterous! It's impossible!" He glanced inquiringly at Mike Riley. "My dear, beautiful girl. You wouldn't do this to me?"

"Oh, yes I would," answered Mike.

Dak Hassan gulped, took a deep breath and recovered his suavity. "Now, my dear girl—and you other people—

consider this matter reasonably. The fifty dollars was a loan, and surely there is nothing criminal in a man's borrowing money from his—" here Dak Hassan had to pause and draw another deep breath, but he finally got the words out "—intended wife?"

Mike Riley gasped unbelievingly. All the other people in the room stared at Dak Hassan. He had the center of the floor again, and he smiled in his old courteously charming way.

"Of course! You see, Miss Riley is my future wife."

"It had better not be very far in the future," Daniels warned.

Dak Hassan made an airy gesture. "I shall attend to it at once—at once." He nodded at Daniels. "You have won, my friend, temporarily. But I have won, too. A million dollars is not so bad, eh?"

Mike Riley started to protest, but Daniels cut her off quickly. "A nice round sum to have," he agreed gravely.

"Come, my dear," Dak Hassan said, taking Mike Riley's arm.

"Oh—Dak Hassan," Daniels said. "I just wanted to tell you something. Did you notice the man lying dead on the path outside?"

"Yes," said Dak Hassan.

"Your future wife just shot him," Daniels said. "She is an excellent pistol shot. That would be a good thing for you to remember."

Dak Hassan's mouth opened a little. He glanced uneasily at Mike Riley. "Interesting," he said, in a subdued voice. "Very interesting. I shall remember it. Come, my dear."

THEY WENT OUT, with Mike Riley pausing in the door-

way for a second to glance back with an expression of startled, unbelieving, frightened happiness on her face.

Cora Sue said uncertainly: "I don't know. I'm worried.
She's so nice and she loves him so much and we owe her
such a great deal and Dak Hassan is—is—"

Daniels chuckled weakly. "Something tells me that Mike
Riley is pretty well capable of handling him. I have an idea
that Dak Hassan is going to make a very good host for a
dude ranch, whether he likes it or not."

"He ought to like it," Biggers said. "She's a swell-looking
girl, although personally I would be a little leary of anybody
who can shoot like she can. I'd hate to have her come after
me with blood in her eye."

"Dak Hassan will be just smart enough to behave himself
for that very reason," Daniels said. "I'll wager that's going
to be an extremely happy marriage." He winked at Cora
Sue. "And I've managed to get rid of one of my rivals."

"Huh?" said Biggers blankly. "Oh. Oh say, what's the
idea about this Mrs. Gregory bringing money for Raker?
What did she do that for?"

"I don't know," Daniels admitted. "We'll have to check
on that. There must be some connection between Mrs.
Gregory and Raker."

There was another altercation at the door, and Foley
came strolling in. He was still wearing his woolly bathrobe,
and he was so drunk that he teetered on his heels. "Hello,
my good people," he said gravely. "Alarums and excur-
sions—shooting, shouting and murder. Are you all alive?"

"More or less," Daniels said.

"How did you get in here?" Biggers demanded.

Foley waved a limp arm. "You forget, my fellow worker,

that I am a deputy-sheriff. I am now investigating this interesting case, and, if I may say so myself, I have made a very vital discovery. I examined the face of our dead friend outside before the coroner took him away. He bears a remarkable resemblance to the former Mrs. Gregory."

"How can you tell?" Biggers demanded skeptically. "Doc Morris made his face all over."

Foley shrugged elaborately. "I don't mean the exterior features of his face. I mean the bony structure. The framework. It is noticeably similar."

Biggers scratched his head. "Charley Raker did have a sister. I've been looking into his case carefully. This sister dropped out of sight ten or fifteen years back when Raker took his first rap. She put up the dough to defend him that time. I've never heard of her since."

"That must be the answer," Daniels said. "Foley, you have a most remarkable ability to identify people. Just how does that come about?"

Foley was wavering back and forth dangerously. "Before I was elevated to my present position of prominence as a gag man, I used to be a cameraman. Cameramen don't just look at a person's face. They look at his features one by one. That's the way you can tell whether a face is photogenic or not. And also, incidentally, it's a very good way to identify a person if you only see one of his features. I think that I will go to sleep now." He suddenly let himself go and fell over backward on the floor with a sodden thump and began to snore instantly.

"Some guy," said Biggers in astonishment.

"As a guest," said Daniels, "he's very easy to entertain. And now I want to make some arrangements with you for tomorrow."

23

THE SHERIFF TAKES HIS MAN

IT WAS CORA SUE who drove Daniels to San Benito the next day, following the path cleared by the county motorcycle police Biggers had assigned to them as an escort, and it was Cora Sue, aided by Jonathan Smythe, the motorcycle policeman, and two court attendants, who protected Daniels from the attentions of the thrill seeking crowd that seethed outside the courthouse.

Daniels was wearing a cast on his right shoulder that bulked hugely clumsy under his coat and shirt. His upper right arm was strapped close against his side, and his forearm was fastened across his chest. His face was pale and sick with pain. He had come over the protests and against the orders of his doctor. But he had come.

He had a driving eagerness to see this thing through, to win against the tremendous odds that were piled against him, and for the first time he believed that he had a chance to do that. If only, weakened and nauseated with pain as he was, he could summon the power and the force he needed.

The courtroom was packed solidly with spectators again, and this time Cora Sue sat at the defense counsel's table beside Daniels, watching him with anxious concern.

When the court was called to order, Boken arose and

said with some reluctance, but with his eye on the reporters who were grouped at a table inside the railing next to
the jury's box:

"Your honor, it has come to the attention of the People
that the counsel for the defense, Mr. Daniels, was gravely
wounded last evening in an effort to protect his wife from
injury at the hands of a notorious criminal. If the defense
wishes to interpose a request for an adjournment at this
time, the prosecution has no objection."

Pooley looked at Daniels. "Mr. Daniels?"

Daniels shook his head slowly. "No. No, thank you.
The defense is ready to proceed at this time, and as our
first witness we wish to call the defendant himself, Peter
Carson, to the stand."

Pete Carson had only the one suit, and it was wrinkled
and soiled from its days of use in the court. His thin face
was alternately white with panic and red with embarrass-
ment as he took the oath. He couldn't control his voice. It
squeaked once, and he brought it back to normal with a
startled gulp. He looked very small sitting in the witness
chair, bewildered and woebegone and scared. He watched
Daniels with the same blind, unreasoning faith that a dog
gives its master.

Daniels stood up.

He was still a little uncertain of his balance, and he had
to steady himself against the defense table before he could
walk across the room. He took his stand in front of the
witness stand, leaning back against the railing that circled
the jury box.

"Pete," he said, thoughtfully, "you know that you have
been on trial for your life here in this courtroom. You know

that I am the only means that you have had with which to
defend yourself. I know that I have done and said a great
many things that you haven't understood, a great many
things that you have had to take on pure blind faith in me,
and yet you never protested or questioned me. Do you still
trust me, Pete?"

"Yes, sir," said Pete, without any hesitation at all.

"Why?" Daniels asked seriously.

Pete wiggled uneasily in the witness chair. "Well—
well—I don't know, Mr. Daniels. It's just the way you
looked at me and talked to me that night up at Phantom
Lake. I don't know..."

"Do you still think that I was right to have you surrendered to the authorities that night?" Daniels inquired.

"Yes, sir."

"Why, Pete?"

"Whatever you say for me to do is right, Mr. Daniels."

"Thank you," said Daniels. "Thank you, Pete. It was right
in this particular case, at least. Now I'm going to prove it.
Your honor, at this point I would like to request that the
court order that no one is to leave the room for the next
hour."

BOKEN SPOKE UP. "Your honor, I am fully aware of the
defense counsel's weakened physical condition, and I have
no desire to further obstruct him, but I must object to this
theatrical hocus-pocus."

"You have a reason for that request, Mr. Daniels?" Pooley
asked, cautiously.

"A very good reason," said Daniels. "So vital a reason
that I think if the request isn't complied with it will reflect
very gravely upon this court." His voice was deadly serious,

and there was no mistaking the fact that he meant exactly what he said.

Pooley blinked and then blinked again and finally nodded at the attendant at the door. "The court orders that no one is to leave this room for any reason for the next hour."

"Thank you," said Daniels. "And now there is one thing more I would like to ask before we start. Are Pappy Hyde and his two sons in this court?"

"You bet they are!" Jonathan Smythe stated emphatically. "Right there!" Pappy and Lee and Jeff Hyde were both in the front row next to the aisle looking suddenly very uneasy and uncomfortable as the attention of the whole room was called to them.

"Thank you," said Daniels again. He turned back toward the witness chair. "Now, Pete, you were present here yesterday when Pappy Hyde testified. Was what he said at that time true?"

"Well—" Pete said uneasily.

"Answer me, Pete, was it true?"

"No, sir," said Pete, "not all of it wasn't."

"Is it true that you spoke scandalously of Dolly Hyde?"

"No!" said Pete emphatically.

"Is it true that you had any immoral intentions toward her?"

Pete's thin face twisted. "No. No, it ain't a bit true! We was gonna get married, just as soon as I could get enough money!"

Daniels nodded. "Pappy Hyde admitted that by implication during his testimony yesterday. He said that he didn't want you in the family. But that's beside the point. Why didn't he want you in the family, Pete?"

Pete started to squirm in the witness chair again. "Well—"

"Why?" said Daniels inexorably. "Tell me why, Pete."

"Well—well, I used to work in a gas station up on the Phantom Lake Road. That ain't so far from the Coldiron Canyon across country. Jeff and Lee and Pappy Hyde, they wanted me to give 'em a little gas."

"Give them gas?" Daniels repeated. "You mean they wanted you to sell them gas?"

"No," said Pete. "They wanted me to give it to 'em."

"Did you own the gas station, Pete?"

"No, sir."

"Well, then, if you gave them gas you would be giving them something that didn't belong to you, wouldn't you? You'd be giving them your employer's gas. You'd have to steal the gas, wouldn't you?"

"Yes, sir," said Pete miserably. "They said I could do it easy, and I guess I could have. There's always some shrinkage and spillage in a gas station, and with a big tank the boss wouldn't miss five or ten gallons, I guess. That's what the Hydes said, anyway. They said there wasn't no chance of me being caught—"

"But you wouldn't do it?"

"No, sir."

"You wouldn't steal for them?"

"No, sir."

"And that's why they got mad at you? That's why they disapproved of your going around with Dolly? Is that it?"

"Yes, sir. They said they wasn't going to have no gutless rabbit in their family."

"I see," said Daniels quietly. He turned around and looked at Boken. "Does the district attorney believe that the defense can't prove without a shadow of a doubt the truth of the testimony the defendant has just given?"

BOKEN'S SQUARE FACE was red as a beet under the stiff pompadour of his hair. He didn't say a word. Daniels turned a little more and faced the audience. "You—Pappy, Lee, and Jeff, stand up!"

The three of them stood up, the two sons tall and gangling and shamefaced beside their shrunken little father.

"Look at them," said Daniels, in the same even quiet tone. "Look at Lee and Jeff Hyde. There are the two men who did not want a brother-in-law who wouldn't steal for them. Look at Pappy Hyde. There is a man who wouldn't let his daughter marry a man who wasn't a thief. There's a man who sat on the stand yesterday and perjured himself, for all of you to hear." His voice suddenly snapped: "I demand here and now that a warrant be issued, and Pappy Hyde arrested for perjury!"

Boken stood up, his face still flushed. "Your honor, no one regrets this occurrence more than I do. I assure you that I had no knowledge that the testimony in question was so biased. I agree that the witness, Pappy Hyde, should be severely censured, but under the circumstances, speaking as he was of a man he believed guilty of his daughter's murder, I think it would be impossible for me to obtain a verdict of perjury."

Daniels was standing up straight now, his weakness

forgotten, and his voice cracked like a whip: "You won't have to worry about that, Mr. Boken, because *you* won't prosecute them! Because *you* won't be the district attorney very much longer! By your stupid stumbling inefficiency you have allowed the completion of the most vicious murder plot of which I have heard! More than that you have *aided* in the plan!

"You sat here and prosecuted an innocent boy, as the murderer knew you would, because he knew what a fool you are! While the murderer himself ran at large and did his bloody deeds without the slightest hindrance from you! He might never have been apprehended except for the brilliant deductive work of your opponent and successor, Jonathan Smythe, sitting *there!*"

Daniels extended his good arm and pointed at Jonathan Smythe, who was staring back in wide-eyed consternation and surprise.

Daniels singled out Sheriff Grimes who was sitting back in a corner on the other side of the judge's dias. "And you, Sheriff! You also aided in this murder plot! You concealed it by running your department with such dimwitted inefficiency that the murderer could have gone on and killed off half the people in this county and you would have never suspected it!

"And he would *be* going on and on now, not even touched with the faintest shadow of suspicion, if it hadn't been for the efforts of the next incumbent of your office, your own deputy-sheriff, Biggers, who worked against your orders, who specifically disobeyed you! Because he did, he solved the murder."

Daniels' voice stopped, and there wasn't another sound

in the court room. Slowly he turned around to look up at Judge Pooley. He didn't say anything, but he frowned in a speculative way.

The skin on Judge Pooley's face looked like unwashed canvas. He tried once, twice and then finally managed a weakly uneasy smile.

Boken suddenly came to life. "I object!"

Pooley cleared his throat, still trying to hang on to his smile. "Mr. Daniels, if you would just go on with your questioning—"

"All right," said Daniels.

Pooley blew out his breath in a long gasp of relief. He looked like a man who had been granted a temporary reprieve from execution.

Daniels nodded at the Hydes. "You can sit down now. Don't try to leave this room."

THE THREE OF them sank back awkwardly in their chairs, vainly trying to avoid the accusing glances of the spectators near them. "Now, Pete," said Daniels, "we'll proceed. Tell the jury just what happened on the day of Dolly's murder."

Pete's hands twisted together uneasily in his lap. "Well—I wanted to see her awful bad—awful bad. So, after work, I sneaked up to her cottage."

"Why?" Daniels asked. "Did you think she wanted to see you?"

"Why, sure," said Pete, surprised.

"Why didn't she come and see you then?" Daniels asked.

"She was afraid. Her brothers and her father, they give her a couple of beatin's for seein' me."

"Nice people, the Hydes," Daniels commented. "Tell me what else happened that day."

"Well, there ain't much else. I went up there and rapped on the back door and there wasn't no answer, and so I opened the door and looked inside and called. And then I seen her—I seen her lyin' there—"

"Yes?" said Daniels. "Yes, Pete?"

"Well—there was blood and I run in and grabbed her, and I seen she was dead—and—and I just went crazy—I couldn't think of nothin' but gettin' help for her—so I went out and run and run and run 'til I found Ham Grey—"

Yes," said Daniels. "That, I think, accounts for all of the testimony that the district attorney has presented. But I want to ask you something else, Pete. I want you to think hard and try to remember now. Do you recall the day of April 2 just four years ago?"

"No, sir," said Pete blankly.

Daniels said: "I will refresh your memory. An accident occurred on that day—a very serious accident."

"Oh, yes. Sure. That was the day Blair Wiles had his accident. Dolly saw it happen.

"Yes, Pete," Daniels said. "Dolly saw it happen. Tell me more about what occurred that day."

"I was workin' in a garage then," Pete said. "A little garage and service station up near the top of Phantom Lake Road."

Daniels interposed a question. "Were you keeping company with Dolly Hyde at that time?"

"Oh, sure," Pete answered. "We been goin' together ever since we was in grade school. Why, on that very day she come up to bring me some cookies that she had baked. It was a pretty long walk for her, but she liked to walk, and it was a nice day. But she dropped the cookies somewhere.

She come runnin' into the garage all hysterical and wanted me to call an ambulance. She said that she had seen Blair Wiles drive off a cliff down the road a ways."

"Did she know Blair Wiles by sight?" Daniels asked. "Well enough to recognize him, I mean?"

"Oh, sure," said Pete. "Everybody knew Mr. Wiles. He had a great big red car, and he was always drivin' fast in it."

"What did Dolly tell you about the accident?"

Pete squinted his eyes, trying to remember. "Well—she was all mixed up and hysterical. She said that she saw Blair Wiles and that stooge of his, go past her real fast in his red car. Blair Wiles was driving. She said that right ahead of her they went off the road and down into a canyon. It was a deep canyon, and she could hear the car crashin' and bangin' all the way down. She was scared stiff, but she run forward and looked down over the edge of the road. She could see the car down there burnin' like everything."

"Go on," requested Daniels. "What else did she say?"

Pete shrugged. "Well, she was all mixed up about it. She said one of 'em was flung free of the car, and that he was crawlin' around and rollin' on the ground and yellin' and that his clothes was all on fire. She said that one was the chauffeur, but of course she was all hysterical and mixed up and got it wrong."

"No, Pete," Daniels said gently. "She didn't get it wrong. She got it right, and because she got it right she was murdered." He turned back toward Judge Pooley. "Your honor, as you will note, it lacks five minutes of being an hour since the time I requested you to order no one to leave the courtroom. I did that because I mean here and now to expose the murderer. He is not in this courtroom, but I did not want to take the chance of anyone getting out and warning him. In exactly five minutes he will come through that door." Daniels pointed toward the front door of the courtroom.

THE TENSION IN the room mounted until it was a crackling, invisible force that pressed down palpably on the brain of every person present.

Daniels stood perfectly still, waiting. There was a long, breathless eternity of suspense. The minute hand crept forward with sly, infinitesimal hesitation, and then it touched the numeral on the dial and covered it. In that second the courtroom doors swung open and the mutter and babble of the crowd outside sounded plainly.

Blair Wiles' wheelchair was pushed into the room, and in it Blair Wiles was a lumpy, blanket-wrapped bundle. His horribly scarred face was dark with blood, and his eye stared with redly distended rage. Biggers was pushing the wheelchair, and over Blair Wiles' grotesque face his own square, commonplace one looked awed and uneasy.

Daniels walked to the gate in the railing and pointed straight down the aisle. "There is the murderer!"

For a moment or two the silence held, breathless and enormous. The wheelchair continued to come on noiselessly; then suddenly it stopped, and that seemed to break the stunned pause.

Boken jumped up incoherent with rage. "Outrage! I protest! I won't stand for this—"

Daniels' voice rode his down. "He is a murderer, and you took money from him for your campaign expenses and so did Sheriff Grimes! Sit down and think up an excuse for that! You'll need it!"

But Boken remained on his feet there. His lips were working, but he could not find words; he could only stare now, his face gone white.

Blair Wiles' voice came thick and choked and low: "You're mad. You're mad, Daniels, but mad or not you'll pay for this! I'll hound you out of the country!"

Pooley finally got up enough courage to speak: "Mr. Daniels, surely you're not suggesting that Blair Wiles— why—why what reason, what possible reason could he have…"

Daniels said: "Blair Wiles could have no reason. Blair Wiles is not guilty of murder. That man is not Blair Wiles. That is Randall, Blair Wiles' ex-chauffeur and bodyguard."

Suddenly his voice rose to an impassioned shout, relentless and logical and unanswerable. "Yes, that man is an imposter! And how ridiculously easy it was for him! Think of it for a second! He didn't have to *look* like the old Blair Wiles, he didn't have to *talk* like the old Blair Wiles, he didn't have to *write* like the old Blair Wiles, he didn't have to *act* like the old Blair Wiles! No! Everyone *expected* him to be different. He had gone through a horrible accident that had supposedly altered him completely!

"Dolly Hyde was right. Randall was thrown clear of the car. He was horribly injured, and his clothes were burned off him. Blair Wiles died in the car, but at the time they were picked up both were so terribly mangled that no one knew which was which. Then Randall was taken to the hospital, and Dr. Morris treated him. Dr. Morris found out that he was Randall, and the idea of the substitution of Randall for Blair Wiles was Dr. Morris' idea.

"Dr. Morris was a crook. Here was a marvelous chance

to make more money than any crook had ever thought of making before. Dr. Morris took it. He persuaded Randall to accept the identity of Blair Wiles. I admit that freely.

"Dr. Morris was the moving force in this thing at the first. It must have been that way. Randall was too seriously injured to have thought up and carried through a plan of this kind. And Dr. Morris continued to be the moving force in the plot and everything went through without the slightest suggestion of a hitch. Randall was accepted by everyone as Blair Wiles—a shadowy, twisted, burned and grotesque Blair Wiles, but nevertheless the real Blair Wiles.

"BUT AS TIME went on, Blair Wiles began to resent his own subordinate position in the plot. Perhaps nothing would have come of that if it had not been for Charles Raker. Now Dr. Morris was, and had been, a crook. He had served criminals before, and once you have gone through that, it is not so easy to drop all contact with your former clients.

"Raker came to Morris and wanted a facial operation, and Morris had to perform it and had to hide him while he was doing so because of the knowledge Raker had about him. That started the whole train of events. Randall liked his position as Blair Wiles and he had no intention of relinquishing it. He knew that Dr. Morris' attention to his criminal clients would sometime later, bring a lot of unwelcome attention to both Dr. Morris and Randall. He wanted to make his own position secure.

The first move was the murder of Dolly Hyde. She was the only witness to the accident. Randall went to talk to her. He had planned it very carefully. Being a cripple and being unable to stand except with the greatest effort, he, of course, sat down. He sat down at the table which Dolly Hyde was setting in the Hyde kitchen. He knew about the Hydes and Pete Carson. He had egged the Hydes on in their treatment of Pete Carson.

"He went to Dolly Hyde as Blair Wiles, as a friend, to talk to her about Pete. That is the criminal, vicious, ruthless part of this. He went as a friend that she trusted offering to help her and Pete. He brought the conversation around to the accident, and he found that she *did* know that it was Randall and not Wiles who had been thrown clear of the car. She had attached no importance to that fact and neither had anyone else. It was thought that she was just hysterical, and the inquiry into the accident was very casual.

"But Randall could take no chances on someone investigating further and believing Dolly Hyde. He murdered her there in the Hyde kitchen, and he left the way he had come, sneaking through the woods up the canyon, fighting his way through the underbrush with his cane, keeping out of sight of Henrietta Parkins.

"Then Pete Carson came as Randall knew he would come and was blamed for the murder as Randall planned that he should be blamed. And because the district attorney was stupid and subservient to the name of Blair Wiles, he aided the murderer in his plan. And because the sheriff was anxious for more campaign contributions from Blair Wiles, he made no effort to really investigate the murder. So that part of the plot went off exactly is it was planned. And then it was time for the next step.

Mrs. Gregory was Raker's sister. He needed money, a

great deal of money, to get himself out of the country safely and to stay under cover when he got out. She brought him that money. Morris knew about it, and he told Randall. Randall killed Mrs. Gregory, and he arranged that murder so it would appear to Raker that Morris had done it.

"He stabbed Mrs. Gregory with Morris' hunting knife, and later he hid the money belt Mrs. Gregory wore in Morris' possession where Raker would find it. Raker *did* think Morris had double-crossed him, and, as a result, he killed Morris just as Randall had planned that he would. And then Raker himself was killed trying to escape, as Randall was sure that he would be. He knew that Raker would never surrender. There was no use in him surrendering. He would have been hung if he had. There then, is the whole pattern completed, and there was no one alive who knew that Randall was Blair Wiles!"

BLAIR WILES TWISTED under his blanket like a swollen, venomous spider. One scarred hand came free, and it was holding a heavy cane. He turned and swung the cane at Biggers' face, and the swish of it going through the air was plainly audible.

Biggers jumped back, ducking, as the cane, unimpeded, struck down across the heavily braced back of the wheel chair and splintered in its center.

Daniels said, "That cane, Randall, isn't quite as strong as the one you murdered Dolly Hyde with."

Randall turned toward him. He clawed his way free of the blankets. He got up and tried to walk toward Daniels. His face was a distorted, writhing smear, and saliva bubbled on his scarred lips. He started falling forward, and the splintered cane was no support.

He sprawled full length in the aisle and all the time his one reddened, distended eye was fixed implacably on Daniels, and he was making thick, mouthing, animal-like sounds in his throat.

For a split second he was there alone on the carpet, clawing like a crippled, enormous bug. Then Biggers and two of the court attendants hurled themselves upon him and merged with him into a scrambling fighting tangle out of which the slobbering, mad animal sounds rose and rose to a crescendo and then died out in choking gasps.

The frantic struggles were stilled now; the quick, harsh breathing of the captors was unnaturally loud, for there was no other sound in the courtroom.

Daniels turned around to face the jury. "Ladies and gentlemen, the defense rests its case."

As if his words were the signal, the room broke into a frenzied uproar, with people scrambling and pushing and fighting for the aisle.

In that first moment, the exhaustion that Daniels had fought off for so long claimed him suddenly. He looked out at the courtroom uproar through a kind of haze; he was aware that his leg was trembling a little. Then he felt an arm supporting him.

Cora Sue was close to Daniels, holding tight to his good arm, and smiling up into his face with an expression that was both proud and worried. Very quickly she led him out through the rear door into the back hall of the courtroom. It was quiet here, suddenly and strangely quiet. Empty because all the loungers had left to participate in the excitement at the front of the court.

Daniels and Cora Sue walked down the hall together

and Daniels said, smiling weakly down at her: "I'm not going to give you any more arguments, dear. I do need a vacation now."

"Oh, no," said Cora Sue. "No more vacation for you. You're going right home and rest up from the rest you've just had." She steered him firmly down the hall toward the door.

www.ingramcontent.com/pod-product-compliance
Lightning Source LLC
Chambersburg PA
CBHW030539030726
47495CB00004B/1054